THE MULTIPLYING MYSTERIES OF MOUNT TEN

THE MULTIPLYING MYSTERIES OF MOUNT TEN

KRISTA VAN DOLZER

BLOOMSBURY
CHILDREN'S BOOKS
NEW YORK   LONDON   OXFORD   NEW DELHI   SYDNEY

BLOOMSBURY CHILDREN'S BOOKS
Bloomsbury Publishing Inc., part of Bloomsbury Publishing Plc
1385 Broadway, New York, NY 10018

BLOOMSBURY, BLOOMSBURY CHILDREN'S BOOKS, and the Diana logo
are trademarks of Bloomsbury Publishing Plc

First published in the United States of America in April 2019
by Bloomsbury Children's Books

Bloomsbury books may be purchased for business or promotional use. For information on
bulk purchases please contact Macmillan Corporate and Premium Sales Department at
specialmarkets@macmillan.com

Library of Congress Cataloging-in-Publication Data
Names: Van Dolzer, Krista, author.
Title: The multiplying mysteries of Mount Ten / by Krista Van Dolzer.
Description: New York : Bloomsbury, 2019.
Summary: When twelve-year-old painter Esther gets stuck at math camp rather than
art camp, she is determined to prove herself but someone leaves cryptic messages
intended to drive her away.
Identifiers: LCCN 2018026351 (print) • LCCN 2018033921 (e-book)
ISBN 978-1-68119-770-8 (hardcover) • ISBN 978-1-68119-773-9 (e-book)
Subjects: | CYAC: Camps—Fiction. | Mathematics—Fiction. | Artists—Fiction. |
Ciphers—Fiction. | Art—Forgeries—Fiction. | Mystery and detective stories.
Classification: LCC PZ7.V2737 Mul 2019 (print) |
LCC PZ7.V2737 (e-book) | DDC [Fic]—dc23
LC record available at https://lccn.loc.gov/2018026351

Book design by Danielle Ceccolini
Typeset by Westchester Publishing Services
Printed and bound in the U.S.A. by Berryville Graphics Inc., Berryville, Virginia
2 4 6 8 10 9 7 5 3 1

All papers used by Bloomsbury Publishing Plc are natural, recyclable products made
from wood grown in well-managed forests. The manufacturing processes conform
to the environmental regulations of the country of origin.

To find out more about our authors and books visit www.bloomsbury.com
and sign up for our newsletters.

For Isaac, Madeleine, and William,
my little number crunchers

THE MULTIPLYING MYSTERIES OF MOUNT TEN

CHAPTER 1

I was lots of things, but outdoorsy wasn't one of them. I could mix paints with my eyes closed and lunge and parry with the best, but when it came to the outdoors, I was as clueless as a brick. Throw in an unexpected downpour and the situation went from bad to deadly.

Unfortunately, Toby was as clueless as I was. He might have looked like a mountain man, with his rosy cheeks and bushy beard, but my stepdad was a city slicker with a taste for alternative rock. I couldn't decide which looked more out of place: his scared, wide-open eyes or his Imagine Dragons shirt.

I squinted through the windshield. The sky was a charcoal-gray canvas slashed through with gnarled black branches and the occasional lightning bolt. "How long is it supposed to rain?"

"All day?" Toby replied, tightening his grip on the steering wheel. It was windy, too. He motioned toward his phone, which he'd stuck in the cup holder. "What does that thing say?"

Eagerly, I scooped up his phone. Mom had finally made him get a real one after he'd dropped his beloved Nokia into a vat of turpentine, but Toby didn't appreciate it like I did. I'd had him convinced that we needed to trade—my phone was so ancient it still had a slide-out keyboard—but Mom had vetoed that idea. She didn't think I needed a new phone until the old one self-destructed.

As luck would have it, Toby's phone looked like it might be on the verge. I could get it to wake up, but even though it was brand-new, none of the apps worked, and the screen kept wigging out.

"It's not saying anything," I said as I returned it to the cup holder.

"Figures," Toby grumbled.

He preferred to communicate with art rather than with deceitful things like words (which could be warped and used against him), so I knew this really meant *You can only trust technology as far as you can throw it.* I'd never had a problem with "newfangled mumbo jumbo," as Toby liked to call it, but he was thirty-five (at least). That was halfway to seventy, and *that* was nearly in the ground.

I fiddled with the radio, but the only station I could get

was the one with that gravelly voiced guy who liked to hear himself make words. "In weather news, torrential rains drench the Wasatch Front," he said before the static cut him off. It was probably just as well. Anyone with two eyes and a window—or even *one* eye and a window—could tell that it was raining. But before I could turn it off, he added, "And it looks like the Fenimore Forger is back in action."

Toby sat up straighter. "Turn it up."

Eagerly, I turned it up, but the station had conked out again. The static was so loud I could hear it over the rain.

Toby slumped back in his seat. "I just wish they'd catch the guy."

Toby and I had been paying close attention to the Fenimore Forger. The story had hit the news when the Fenimore Art Museum announced that one of their recent acquisitions, a lesser-known Thomas Cole, had turned out to be a fake. The museum had traced the painting's roots, but they'd turned out to be as tangled as my hair in a windstorm. Apparently, the Fenimore Forger never stayed in one place long enough for the authorities to track him down. He came, he painted, and he left.

"I hope they catch him, too. Or *her*. It could be a girl, you know. Artists come in all shapes and sizes."

Toby rumpled my hair. "Yes, they do."

Pride glowed in my chest, a ray of warmth on this gray day, but instead of letting it distract me, I set my sights on the clouds. "I hope the rain doesn't interfere with the Jackson Pollock workshop."

Camp Vermeer, which billed itself as "the only week-long camp your artist will ever need," required applicants to submit detailed portfolios, so I'd tried not to get my hopes up. Mr. Nelson, my art teacher, had helped me take pictures of the pieces I'd been working on in class, but the *pièce de résistance*—that was French for the best part—was the collection of campaign materials I'd produced for my friend David, our new seventh-grade class president. He'd won the election thanks to those campaign materials, and Director Saffron, Camp Vermeer's respected owner, had also been impressed. She'd called Shiny David, a life-size sculpture I'd constructed from dozens of broken mirror pieces on a welded wire frame, "a mixed-media sensation." She'd even liked the T-shirts David and I had created by allowing our classmates to fire real, live paintballs at us. If I remembered right, she'd used the word "ingenious."

Toby grunted his agreement. "And I hope it's not much farther."

I sincerely hoped that, too, but when we rounded the next bend, we didn't catch a glimpse of Camp Vermeer, just another stretch of winding road. Not ten feet in front of us, it dipped down into a gully that currently looked more like a creek with so much water gushing through it. I might not have known much about the great outdoors, but anyone who'd played in gutters knew it didn't take a lot of water to make objects float downstream.

I sent Toby a sideways glance. "You think we can get across?"

"Doubtful," he replied. When he tried to shift into reverse, the truck's gears shrieked in complaint, and we rolled forward, not backward.

Toby and I weren't natural screamers, but that didn't mean my heart couldn't pound out of control. While he pumped the brake, I braced myself against the dashboard and tried to remember how to breathe. Luckily, the truck only skidded a few feet before it crashed into a boulder on the far side of the road.

For a long time, we just sat there, catching up on breaths we'd missed. Finally, Toby asked, "Okay?"

I patted myself down. "All body parts accounted for." I glanced at him. "What about you?"

"I'm fine," he said curtly, though he would have said that even if his femur had been sticking out of his thigh. I knew what femurs were thanks to Toby's *Atlas of Human Anatomy for the Artist* (which I'd been sneaking peeks at since I was nine). "But the truck's seen better days."

I tested my door, which was now wedged against the boulder. "Are we really stuck?" I asked.

Toby looked around. "For now."

"Well, then, we'd better ditch the truck." There was no way one measly boulder was going to keep me from Camp Vermeer. "I've got some ponchos in the back."

I'd planned on using them for the Jackson Pollock workshop, but sometimes you had to improvise. Rain pelted my face as I wrestled open the back window and burrowed under the tarp. It smelled like moldy plastic and was wetter than something waterproof had a right to be, but I'd crawl under a thousand tarps that smelled like moldy plastic to get to Camp Vermeer. When I emerged a few minutes later with a pair of matching ponchos, I felt nothing but triumphant.

He glanced at the ponchos, then at the water pouring down the windshield. "You really want to go out there?"

"Well, we can't stay here," I said. "I didn't know we might get stuck, so I only brought one pack of Corn Nuts."

He nodded toward the gully. "How do we get across *that*?"

I stuck out my chin. "We jump." I wasn't familiar with flash floods, but since Toby wasn't, either, I could afford a little overconfidence.

He considered that, then shrugged. "I guess we won't last long on Corn Nuts." After unfolding his poncho, he pulled it over his head.

I unfolded mine, too. Now that we were definitely going out there, I had to admit that I was nervous. I glanced back at the tarp, stalling. "Should we bring my stuff or leave it here?"

"Leave it here," Toby replied. "I'll come back for it later."

He glanced up at the clouds—*You can't keep raining forever*, his grim expression seemed to say—then pushed open his door and slowly slid out of the truck. I slithered out behind him. I'd barely taken a step before my shoes were caked with mud, but at least the rest of me was dry. The last thing I wanted to do was waltz into Camp Vermeer, which was half-boys and half-girls, with wet clothes and soggy hair.

"This way," Toby said as he skidded down the shoulder to the gully. He gestured toward the logs that had wedged themselves between the boulder and the gully's other bank. "We'll cross the water on these logs. If you feel yourself start to slip, try to grab those branches over there."

He pointed at a low-lying limb that bowed over the road, and I couldn't help but gulp. I was tall, but not that tall. If I started to slip, I'd have a better chance of suddenly learning how to fly than of grabbing that limb. I slid one toe onto the logs, but before I could take the plunge (metaphorically speaking), Toby grabbed hold of my arm.

"Maybe you should let me go first."

I yanked my toe back. "Be my guest."

After adjusting his poncho, Toby climbed onto the thickest log, which didn't even tremble. Slowly, very slowly, he pushed his front foot forward, then dragged his back foot behind it. I stuck both hands on my hips as I watched him inch his way across. It was going to take forever at this rate. But he did reach the other side, so I guess his patience paid off.

"Your turn," he said quietly.

I took a deep breath. If Toby could make it across, then I was sure that I could, too. I licked my lips, then clambered up onto the log that hadn't even quaked for Toby. It sat slightly higher than the others, so it wasn't as slippery as I'd expected, but it also wasn't as stable. Toby's crossing must have weakened it.

Luckily, I had tricky feet.

I didn't wait for it to settle, just raced across the makeshift bridge, curling the soles of my broken-in shoes around the bumpy, grumpy log. If there was one thing I'd picked up from seven years of fencing lessons, it was that footwork was the most important part. I was one hop, skip, and a jump away from the other bank when my toe caught on a knot. My arms pinwheeled spectacularly, and before I knew it, I was plunging into the creek.

But I never hit the water. Somehow, a branch had snagged my poncho, leaving me high and (somewhat) dry.

Toby grabbed me by my collar and dragged me over to his side. "Esther," he said softly. He never talked in exclamation points, but I could tell that he was worried. He got quieter when he was nervous.

"I'm fine," I said through gritted teeth, wiggling my toes experimentally. "But I think I just lost a toenail."

Usually, he liked to sketch non-life-threatening injuries for posterity, but since he didn't have his sketchbook, Toby thumped me on the back. I immediately felt better. When he headed up the road, I didn't hesitate to follow.

As we trudged up the muddy road, I remembered this story I'd once heard about a kid who climbed a mountain by placing his feet in his dad's footprints, but Toby's footprints didn't stick around long enough for me to fill them. As soon as he lifted his foot, the mud swallowed the outline of his shoe. It must have been doing the same thing to my footprints, but I was too tired to check. It was taking everything I had to keep myself moving forward.

When we reached the next bend in the road, there was no Camp Vermeer, but there was a sign:

CAMP ARCHIMEDES   1/2 MILE

"Camp Archimedes?" I blurted. "It's supposed to be Camp Vermeer."

Toby wiped the rain out of his eyes. "Maybe they just changed the name."

That didn't sound likely to me, but I was too worn out to challenge him. "Maybe," I admitted. "And at least we know it's only another two thousand, six hundred"—I paused to calculate—"and forty feet, right?"

Toby arched an eyebrow.

"Never mind," I said. "Let's just think of it as half a mile."

Except a half mile in thick mud was a heck of a lot different than on a level track. By the time a fence came into sight, it felt like centuries had passed. I was so wet that I'd forgotten what it felt like to be dry. The poncho was less of a rain deflector than a sweat holder-inner.

"Come on," Toby said when I nearly tripped over a tree root. I wasn't usually so clumsy, but then, I wasn't usually so wet. "Looks like we're nearly there."

Except "there" didn't look much like the photos on the website. There were supposed to be a bunch of cabins, but there was just one lodge instead. And it was the biggest lodge I'd ever seen. If Harry Potter had been a lumberjack, this place could have been Hogwarts. It was shaped like a backward L and thirty or forty feet tall, with a steep roof, gabled windows, and an oak door with iron hinges. The sign that spanned the driveway said CAMP ARCHIMEDES again.

"This isn't right," I mumbled.

"What's not right?" he asked.

"*That,*" I said emphatically as I motioned toward the lodge. "It's not supposed to be so . . . big. And there's supposed to be a mural."

Toby smoothed his beard. "We're standing in front of a log castle and you're griping?" he replied.

I scowled down at my shoes. I guess he had a point. But

if they didn't have that Jackson Pollock workshop, I was going to ask for a refund.

We were halfway up the walk that connected the road to the lodge when the door flew open with a *bang* and a woman materialized on the porch. Director Saffron's photo hadn't been on the website, but I'd been picturing her as a free spirit, a female version of Toby. As it turned out, "free" and "spirit" were two of the last words I would have used to describe this slick-haired, high-heeled woman.

"May I help you?" she asked primly. She was trying not to shout, but the thunder made that hard.

I pointed a thumb at my chest. "My name is Esther Lambert, and this is my stepdad, Toby Renfro. He's here to drop me off."

"Esther Lambert?" she replied. "I don't have a camper by that name."

I forced myself not to snort. Did she really have the list of campers *memorized*? Apparently, the camp was a lot less well-attended than I'd been led to believe. I was about to say so, too, when the door opened again and a pack of scrunch-faced boys appeared. You would have thought they'd never seen the sun from the way they were blinking.

The woman cleared her throat. "Perhaps you'd like to come inside," she said as she stepped out of the way. "You look positively saturated."

Positively saturated? Who stuck those two words together?

"Thank you," Toby huffed as he plodded up the steps.

But I wasn't giving in without a fight. "This *is* Camp Vermeer, isn't it?"

The woman shook her head. "Oh, no, it's Camp Archimedes, home of the world-famous Crazy Cryptography course. Didn't you see the signs?"

"But it used to be Camp Vermeer." When she didn't react, I added, "And it's still an art camp, right?"

"An art camp?" she replied. If she hadn't said "positively saturated," I might have thought she was a parrot. "Oh, dear, this is quite the predicament."

Adrenaline coursed through my veins. "What do you mean, 'oh, dear'?"

The woman pursed her lips. "I hate to be the bearer of bad news, but I'm afraid Camp Archimedes is, in fact, a math camp."

CHAPTER 2

Her words rang in my ears like the deep *thrum* of a gong. I'd ended up at a *math* camp? Did math camps even exist?

The woman waved us into the lodge. "Please make yourselves comfortable."

"But I don't want to come in." I stumbled back instinctively. "I'm not supposed to even be here."

The woman flashed her teeth, not quite a grin or a grimace. "Well, you *are* here, so that's that."

"*Esther,*" Toby said.

He only said my name in italics when I was pushing the limits of his patience (which was usually limitless), but I pretended not to notice. "I bet Camp Vermeer is over there." I motioned vaguely up the road. "It's just past that dead tree, right?"

She motioned back the way we'd come. "You see that mountain through those trees?"

The road provided enough of a break that I could catch a glimpse of a distant summit. Thanks to the pouring rain, it looked fuzzy and washed-out—it could have been a cloud as easily as it was a mountain—but I nodded anyway.

"Camp Vermeer is over *there*," she said (smugly, if you asked me). She pulled down a map on a roller; I recognized the interstate but not any of the numbered mountains. "We like to call that one Mount Seven. We like to call this one Mount Ten."

I sucked a sharp breath through my teeth. "You mean we went up the wrong mountain?"

She nodded ruefully. "And the drive back down *this* mountain would take at least several hours, and that's in the best of weather."

I fought the urge to glare at Toby. It wasn't his fault that he didn't know northeast from southwest.

Or maybe it was.

The woman stepped out of the way. "Are you ready to come in?"

I didn't nod exactly, but then, I didn't have to. Without another word, the woman shooed the other kids back into the gloomy lodge. They were waiting for us in a half circle when we finally emerged into the common room's dim glow. We just stood there dripping, and they just stood there gawking. We would have made a great still life.

The math nerds looked pale and chalky, but that could have been the mist that somehow hung over the room. Most were frighteningly short, but two were on the taller side, one with fiery red hair and the other with black. There were ten campers in all, only two of whom were girls. One of them looked picture-perfect, with long blond hair and flawless skin, but the other girl looked normal. If she hadn't been glaring at me, I would have pegged her as a friend.

Behind them were the woman and three younger counselors (two men and one woman), and behind *them* were the chalkboards, walls and walls of chalkboards (which explained the mist). I hadn't thought that anyone used chalkboards anymore, but based on the variety of scribbles, it was probably safe to say that *everyone* at Camp Archimedes used them. And it wasn't like these nerds were practicing their long division. I hadn't known math could involve so many letters.

"Forgive us for intruding," Toby said after he coughed.

"Nonsense," the woman said. "Oh, but where are my manners?" She offered her hand to Toby. "My name is Director Verity."

"Toby Renfro," Toby said.

"And I'm still Esther," I replied.

Director Verity forced a smile (or at least it looked forced to me). "It's very nice to meet you. Would you like something to drink?"

Toby looked down at his poncho. "I think I'd just like a bathroom."

"Oh, of course," she said, nodding toward the hall that extended down the lodge's shorter leg. "It's the fourth door on the right. If you reach the full-size gym, then you'll know you've gone too far."

Toby nodded back, then crossed the dusty common room, leaving a trail of mud and twigs. When he disappeared down the dark corridor, I couldn't help but feel alone.

Ten pairs of eyes latched on to me, and mine couldn't help but gape at them. If they looked like wide-eyed aliens, I could only imagine what I looked like.

Before the silence could get awkward (or *more* awkward, anyway), the director chirped, "Number crunchers, introduce yourselves to our newest arrival."

She made it sound like I was staying, but I most certainly was *not*. As soon as this storm died down, we would hike back to the truck and skedaddle out of here. After we fixed it, of course, but that wouldn't take long. Toby was a whiz with metal.

The math nerds mumbled their names one by one, but I couldn't hear most of them above the pounding rain. I did manage to catch the blond-haired girl's (Angeline) and the fiery redhead's (Graham), but that was just because the wind died down during their turns.

Director Verity beamed. "Thank you, number crunchers. You may return to your prime-factor trees."

I glanced at their prime-factor trees (which seemed too simple for this crowd), then did an instant double take. They were prime-factoring numbers in the ten and hundred *thousands*. I was still checking their math when Toby emerged from the bathroom. He'd shed the less-than-helpful poncho, but his shirt was still completely soaked, and the bottoms of his jeans were caked in multicolored mud.

Director Verity took one look at him and glanced at one of the male counselors. "It looks like our guests could both use a change of clothes. Mr. Pearson, you appear to be Mr. Renfro's size. May we borrow some of yours?"

Mr. Pearson disappeared down the other corridor without saying a word.

Next, she sized me up, then turned her attention to the glaring girl. "Brooklyn, the same request?"

The glaring girl, whose pale white skin was even paler than skim milk, went right on glaring at me. "I don't have a change of clothes."

That wasn't something I'd admit in front of the other campers. The black-haired boy smiled—he must have been thinking the same thing—but I didn't smile back. I was only going to be here for a few hours at most. I didn't need to make new friends.

"I do!" Angeline chirped. For a second, maybe less, she sounded exactly like Director Verity.

I opened my mouth to tell them that they didn't need to worry, that we wouldn't be here long enough for our clothes to dry out, but Director Verity didn't let me get a word in edgewise.

"Thank you, Angeline," she said, and from the way that she was beaming, I could tell Angeline was her favorite.

Angeline followed Mr. Pearson, leaving Toby and me to stew in our own smelly juices—until Director Verity took it upon herself to distract us. She would have made a great detective, since she never ran out of questions: "What do you do?" "Where are you from?" "What made you want to go to Camp Vermeer?" "Would you like some hot chocolate?" Toby answered her questions with his usual grunts and three-word explanations, and I tried to follow suit. She wasn't going to get any tidbits out of me.

Angeline and Mr. Pearson reappeared at the same time, bearing bundles of folded clothes. It looked like Toby and Mr. Pearson were roughly the same size, but when I held up Angeline's pants (which were sparkly, no less), they looked two inches too short.

"Too bad," Toby said simply. "I guess beggars can't be choosers."

I didn't bother to respond. Toby never let me sulk.

He motioned toward the bathroom. "Do you want to change first?"

I glanced at the sparkly pants, then at my soggy poncho. Though I was still sopping wet, I shook my head. I didn't want to change until I absolutely had to.

"Suit yourself," he said, then retreated to the bathroom. When the door slammed shut behind him, chalk dust swirled in the air.

I bounced my foot up and down, ignoring the way that my shoes squelched. I looked over at the window, hoping against hope that the storm was blowing itself out, but the rain was still coming down in sheets. I returned my attention to my shoes.

"The storm shouldn't relent for another few days," Director Verity said. It was like she'd read my mind. "Perhaps you'd like that drink now?"

Instead of fighting her, I nodded. I was cold and tired. The last thing I wanted to do was match wits with a grown-up math nerd.

Director Verity nodded back, then disappeared down the same corridor Angeline and Mr. Pearson had. That drew my attention to a nearby chalkboard. It was the only chalkboard in the room that had just one person's handwriting (and judging by the loops and frills, that person was probably Director Verity).

It must have been a problem of some sort, but it didn't look like any problem I'd ever come across. I got up to examine it, but it made no more sense up close than it had from far away:

You walk into a room with three sets of balanced scales.

On the first scale, two red balls and one blue ball balance with two yellow balls and a one-pound weight.

On the second scale, four red balls and a one-pound weight balance with one blue ball and one yellow ball.

On the third scale, one red ball and two yellow balls balance with one blue ball and one yellow ball.

How much does each ball weigh?

"It's the camp's First Problem," a deeper voice said from behind me.

I glanced over my shoulder. Graham, the fiery redhead, was suddenly headed my way.

"If someone solves this one, they'll supposedly move on to the next. But if someone solves the First, I told Marshane I'd lick his shoes." He tilted his head to the side, accentuating the contrast between his red hair and light skin. "I don't think 'challenging' even begins to describe it."

I crinkled my nose. If *Graham* thought it was challenging, I wouldn't stand a chance—and that left me no choice but to shoot it full of holes. "How do the balls stay on the scales? I mean, wouldn't they roll off?"

"I guess they would, wouldn't they?" Graham considered that, then shrugged. "Maybe it's just a hypothetical."

I had no idea what a hypothetical was, but I liked the way it sounded, like a poem in one word. "Then maybe the answer is, too." And with that, I sauntered off.

I was halfway to an empty bench when Toby emerged from the bathroom. Mr. Pearson's sweater was too tight— apparently, he didn't make a habit of hauling scrap metal around—but at least it didn't sparkle. After exchanging a look with Toby, I grabbed Angeline's clothes, then shuffled down the hall to this mysterious bathroom.

It was smaller than I'd expected, given the size of the lodge, but at least it didn't smell like pee. I fumbled for the light switch, but nothing happened when I flicked it, so I tried a few more times.

The light switch still didn't work.

Icy wisps of dread chased me back out to the common room. "The lights are dead!" I said to no one in particular.

Director Verity looked up. "Yes, I'm afraid the power's out."

My gaze darted up to the antler chandelier dangling from the vaulted ceiling (which was flickering alarmingly, but then, it *was* flickering).

She had the decency to blush. "Oh, well, there's a generator."

I narrowed my eyes. If they had a generator, why weren't *all* the lights working?

"But it's only connected to the common rooms," she said.

"How convenient," I replied. Something wasn't adding up.

She produced a red Maglite out of nowhere. "Would you like to borrow my flashlight?"

I gaped at the sturdy Maglite, which was as long as her forearm, then at her bloodred nails. What kind of outdoorswoman coordinated her nails with her Maglite? And why did she need one so *big*?

"Oh, no, that's all right," I said as I slithered back a step. "I can just . . . open the blinds."

Not my cleverest excuse, since it was gray and overcast, but Director Verity just nodded.

"Good idea," she said, returning her Maglite to its holster. "Best to save the batteries for the witching hour later."

A shiver tiptoed down my spine. I didn't want to think about how dark it was going to get. With no power. In the rain.

After retreating to the bathroom and double-checking the cheap lock, I shucked off my poncho and wriggled out of my wet clothes. Angeline hadn't thought to bring another pair of shoes, so I scraped as much mud off mine as I could, then turned them upside down over the vent. Bare feet were best, anyway, especially in summer storms.

After wringing out my explosion of red hair, I unlocked the door. I hadn't been able to hear what was going on, but as soon as I reentered the common room, I shuddered to a stop. It didn't take a brainiac to know something was up.

For one thing, Toby was nursing a steaming mug of hot chocolate (even though he usually said hot chocolate tasted like bathwater), and for another, Director Verity was laughing like he'd just said something very funny. I thought Toby was hilarious, but most people found him weird. And the last time I checked, Director Verity didn't laugh. When she said, "I guess that's settled," I rushed into their conversation.

"What's settled?" I demanded.

"Why, your stay at Camp Archimedes, home of the world-famous Crazy Cryptography course." She offered me a hot chocolate. "We're so happy to have you, Esther."

CHAPTER 3

I ignored the hot chocolate. My gaze flickered back and forth between Toby and Director Verity. "I'm *staying*?" I replied.

Toby's cheeks turned red, but he didn't bother to correct her, just took a swig of his hot chocolate.

At least Director Verity was willing to look me in the eyes. "Well, of course you are!" she said. "We can't have you drowning in that creek, and your vehicle is out of commission."

"I'm sure it just needs a push." I motioned toward the counselors (who probably didn't have much experience with manual labor, but we'd take what we could get). "Maybe they could dig us out?"

Director Verity shook her head. "It's too dangerous," she said. "From what Mr. Renfro tells me, the road is nigh unto impassable."

"We passed it, didn't we?" I growled.

She didn't comment on my tone. "Be that as it may, your stepfather and I have both decided that you should stay here for the time being, at least until the rain subsides."

"Easy for *you* to say," I said, glaring at Toby's hot chocolate (since I couldn't bring myself to glare at him). "You're not the one who has to stay—"

"I don't think you understand," she interrupted. "Mr. Renfro will be staying, too."

That was something, anyway. And as Mom was fond of saying, the weather in this part of Utah liked to change every five minutes, so with any luck, we'd be digging out the truck and showing Camp Archimedes our tailpipe in no more than an hour.

"Now, let's get you two settled," Director Verity went on. "Mr. Renfro can bunk in Cabin Beta with Mr. Sharp and Mr. Pearson, and you can room in Cabin Epsilon with Brooklyn and Angeline."

I narrowed my eyes. "I thought we couldn't go outside."

"Oh, well, they're not actual cabins," Director Verity replied. "And I'm sure Brooklyn and Angeline will be thrilled to have another roommate."

Brooklyn sniffed dismissively, but Angeline's eyes sparkled. In general, I tried to avoid people who sparkled in any way, but if we'd be sharing a room, I'd have a hard time dodging her.

Director Verity clapped. "Let's stretch those muscles!" she

went on. "As every number cruncher knows, having healthy hearts and lungs is key to having healthy minds."

The math nerds groaned in unison, but I couldn't decide whether they disliked exercise or Director Verity's one-liners. As they plodded down the hall that led away from the bathroom, I had no choice but to follow.

The hall on the right was narrower than the one on the left. After we trudged past a closed door with a nameplate that said DIRECTOR VERITY, the corridor opened up into another giant room that was clearly the mess hall. Except calling it a mess hall was like calling this place a lodge. On the right was a gourmet kitchen complete with granite and stainless steel, and on the left was a dining room that could have seated several hundred. In the middle was a woodburning fireplace with a redwood-size chimney that sprouted from the floor and disappeared into the ceiling. A bridge made of planks and logs wrapped around it from both sides, connecting two sections of the lodge's second floor.

It was the single most amazing room that I'd ever encountered, and I had a sudden itch to sketch it. But I'd left my sketchbook in the truck, so I snapped a quick picture instead. Then I scurried to catch up.

We'd just entered the next corridor when the director made a sharp left turn and headed up a hidden staircase. Weak light dribbled through a skylight, and the steps creaked ominously. I gripped the gnarled banister, which looked like a sawed-off branch, and curled my toes around each step.

At the top of the stairs, Director Verity stopped near the first doors, which were labeled CABIN ALPHA and CABIN BETA. "Your room, Mr. Renfro," she said dramatically as she opened Cabin Beta's door.

I crowded in behind the others to get a look inside his room, but it was mostly disappointing. Instead of four-poster beds with silky sheets, there were plain bunks with fleece blankets. Also, it smelled like canned tuna.

"Mr. Sharp and Mr. Pearson have already claimed their spaces," Director Verity went on, "but I'm sure you'd be more than welcome to any of the remaining bunks."

Toby dipped his head, but before he slipped inside, he glanced back at me. "Are you sure you'll be all right?"

The math nerds' beady eyes zoomed in on me like double periscopes, and I swallowed, hard. I'd never been a clingy kid, but the thought of being without Toby in this creepy-crawly place was enough to make me sweat. I'd had this perfect plan of how everything would turn out, but so far, none of it had worked.

Still, I couldn't lose it, not in front of these math nerds. They already thought I was an alien from the planet Creativity, so I ducked my head and mumbled, "Yeah."

Toby dipped his head again. "Then I'll catch up with you at dinner."

He vanished before I could say goodbye, but that was probably just as well. At least when the door closed, it took the smell of tuna with it.

Director Verity raised a hand. "Onward, my little number crunchers!"

The math nerds scampered after her, plunging across another bridge. Raindrops dripped off my fat curls, peppering my borrowed shirt as I hurried to catch up.

Angeline must have thought I was crying, because she bumped my arm and said, "I'm sure he's going to be fine."

Behind us, Brooklyn snorted. "Can it, Angeline," she said, pushing past us with a sneer. "I bet Camp Archimedes is going to eat this one alive."

I opened my mouth to answer, but she didn't wait for me to finish (or even give me a chance to start), just flicked her hair over her shoulder and half tromped, half tripped away. Reluctantly, we followed.

"Don't mind her," Angeline said. She had to take two steps for every single one of mine. "Brooklyn is just feeling homesick."

I stared at Brooklyn's fists. She didn't look homesick to me, but then, I didn't know what homesickness looked like. "If you say so," I said.

Angeline nodded knowingly. "I see it all the time."

"How long have you been here?" I asked.

Angeline ducked her head. "Well, it's my first time at *this* camp. But I've been to lots of others, like Camp Einstein, Camp Newton"—she ticked them off on her fingers—"and the Jolly Jamboree."

I couldn't help but grin. "You totally made that last one up."

"No, I didn't!" she replied, but then she ducked her head again. "Okay, maybe I did. But the Peace Pirates are my crew, and every time we get together, it's a jolly jamboree."

I made a face. "Your crew?"

"Yeah, you know, my hip-hop crew."

I clapped a hand over my mouth so I wouldn't laugh out loud. If she wanted to play make-believe, that was her business, not mine.

After crossing the same bridge the math nerds had just scampered over (which spanned a fully loaded game room complete with pool, Ping-Pong, air hockey, and a bunch of old arcade games), we passed two more doors that looked exactly like Toby's, though these ones were labeled CABIN GAMMA and CABIN DELTA.

"The boys' rooms," Angeline said. "They're not allowed to come in ours, and we're not allowed to go in theirs, but honestly, who'd want to?"

As if on cue, one of the math nerds tumbled out the door marked CABIN GAMMA, a candy wrapper stuck to his shoe. He must have snuck in for a snack while Director Verity's back was turned.

Angeline arched an eyebrow. *See what I mean?* it seemed to ask.

I covered my mouth to hide my grin. Maybe these math nerds weren't so awful after all.

When we reached the last two doors (CABIN EPSILON and CABIN ZETA), Director Verity finally stopped. "Welcome to your home away from home, Esther!"

I shook my head ferociously. "I don't need a home away from home. Only until the storm dies down, remember?"

The director forced a nervous chuckle. "Oh, yes, until the rain subsides." But she wouldn't meet my eyes. "We should let you get settled in. Number crunchers, back downstairs! I think I feel a game of Math Genius coming on."

I forced myself not to shiver. Why did I get the impression she was lying to my face?

Angeline hopped forward a step. "Is it all right if I keep Esther company?"

Director Verity pursed her lips. "If it's all right with Esther," she replied.

I considered that, then shrugged. "I guess it's okay with me." It wasn't like I needed help unpacking, but after everything she'd done, I owed her an excuse to get out of playing Math Genius.

Angeline smiled. "You're welcome!"

"Thank you," I mumbled as she skipped into the room.

I waited for the math nerds to disappear, then reluctantly

trudged after Angeline. Cabin Epsilon didn't smell like tuna, but it was almost as depressing. Shadows clung like cobwebs to the corners of the room, and though it could have slept an army, it only had three lousy bunks. That meant the room had six beds total, all of which were a boring brown. The floorboards were brown, too, as were the walls and ceiling. It was like I'd moved into a chocolate factory—minus the chocolate. There *was* a sliding door that led onto a balcony, but the view was dreary: rain, rain, and more rain.

Two of the six beds had already been claimed by other campers, and it wasn't hard to tell whose bed was whose. The one closest to the door was covered in a puffy pink blanket while the one closest to the wall sported the standard-issue green. I tried not to hold Angeline's awful tastes against her.

Angeline spread out her arms. "What do you think?" she asked.

I took another look around. She obviously loved this place, and I didn't want to make her feel bad. "I think it's brown," I said.

If she picked up on my indifference, she didn't bother to show it. "Which bed do you want?" she asked, motioning vaguely toward the other bunk. Before I had a chance to answer, she whirled around, her blue eyes wide. "Unless you want to share with me? I've heard the top is extra comfy."

I couldn't hold my hands up fast enough. "Oh, no, that's

all right." I racked my brains for an excuse. "I have a fear of . . . ladders."

Angeline looked down at her toes. "Oh, okay. I understand." She must have known that I was lying, but she didn't call my bluff, just gestured toward the empty bunk. "Sheets and blankets on the beds."

Guilt squirmed in my stomach like an old bologna sandwich, but I pretended not to notice. I wasn't here to make best friends; I was here to get a good night's sleep and go. Camp Vermeer was calling, and I intended to answer.

CHAPTER 4

The rain didn't let up as the afternoon wore on. The world beyond my window looked like a Monet in black and white, with fuzzy lines and shapes melting from one gray into another. Every once in a while, a lightning bolt would split the sky, illuminating a collage of trees, and I would race to snap a picture. You couldn't get these kinds of shots down in the valley where I lived.

I tucked my hands behind my head and lay back on my lumpy mattress. Angeline kept trying to get me to go downstairs, but I kept ignoring her. There were only so many ways you could say you didn't want to play Math Genius.

Finally, she gave up and left. I wasn't sad to see her go. The peace and quiet was refreshing, but as the minutes stretched to *more* minutes, I had to admit that I was bored.

I groped under my bed for the corner of my sketchbook,

but my fingers came up empty. It took me a few moments to remember where it was. Sighing, I flopped back on the bunk and tried to let myself drift off. But I was too wound up to sleep.

Just because I wasn't staying didn't mean that I couldn't explore.

I poked my head out into the hall, an excuse dancing on my tongue in case they tried to rope me into doing something with someone, but happily, the hall was empty. Voices were drifting up from somewhere, but no one was in sight, so I eased the door shut behind me. The sparkly pants wouldn't make great camouflage, but they would have to do.

No one was in the sitting room below our room, so I skulked across that bridge without running into trouble, but the closer I got to the next bridge, the louder the voices became. When I peeked over the railing, I easily spotted the math nerds in the afternoon's gray light. Armed with compasses and protractors, they were huddled around the pool table while the female counselor prattled on about angles of reflection and Mr. Sharp polished his cue. It looked like they were measuring the angles at which the balls bounced off the rails.

Honestly, they were in a game room, surrounded by every waste of time anyone had ever invented, and they were *measuring angles*? It was like they'd spent their whole lives locked up in some scientist's lab, and now that they'd finally broken out, they'd fallen back into another. Someone really needed to teach them how summer camps were supposed to be.

But it wasn't going to be me.

While Mr. Sharp lined up his shot, I snapped a picture of the scene. As soon as his elbow jerked forward, I raced across the exposed bridge, using the chimney as a shield. I'd almost made it to the other side when I glanced over my shoulder and noticed Brooklyn watching me. Or it looked like she was watching me. But she didn't rat me out, just went back to her measurements. She must have disliked my company as much as I disliked hers.

When I got to Toby's room, I almost knocked twice on the door, then changed my mind at the last second. Mr. Pearson might be in there, and I wasn't in the mood to explain what I was up to.

The stairwell was also empty, but that wasn't much of a surprise. In a lodge this big—and with a group of kids this small—most of the living spaces were bound to be unoccupied. Still, I hugged the walls so the stairs wouldn't be tempted to creak. Director Verity hadn't said that I couldn't leave my room, but I didn't want to push her.

The mess hall sounded empty, too, but when I rounded the next corner, I nearly crashed into Mr. Pearson. We both leaped out of the way, but he was the one who lost his grip on the stewed tomatoes he'd been stirring. The bowl hit the floorboards with a *clang*, splattering the tomatoes and their juices all over the floor and the bottoms of his slacks.

"I'm so sorry," I mumbled, getting down to clean it up. I couldn't do much without a rag, but I *could* scoop the stewed tomatoes back into their silver bowl. "I didn't see you there."

"It was my fault," he mumbled back (though he didn't help with the tomatoes). "I shouldn't have been sneaking."

"You were sneaking?" I replied as I glanced around the kitchen. Cutting boards and mixing bowls were haphazardly spread out on the counter. Either he was making dinner, or I was missing something crucial.

"Never mind," Mr. Pearson said, jerking the bowl out of my hands.

I couldn't help but notice his nails, which were dotted with red flecks. "You're a painter!" I replied. I sounded like a hopeless groupie.

Mr. Pearson glanced down at his hands, then shook his head and wiped them on his apron. "It must be the tomato," he mumbled.

I felt my shoulders fall. "Oh, right." I felt extra bad for bumping into him—and for accusing him of being a painter. He'd probably assumed it was an insult. "Do you need help with dinner? I'm pretty handy with a knife."

He shook his head again. "But thanks."

His thanks sounded more like, *And don't ever speak to me again*, but I tried not to take it personally. I got the impression that he didn't like to work with people (or even talk to them).

"I guess I'll go, then," I mumbled as I headed toward the common room. I was halfway to the corridor when I realized I might look suspicious. "Director Verity wanted to talk."

But he wasn't listening anymore—he'd gone back to his tomatoes—and that was just as well. Director Verity's office was in sight of the kitchen, and I didn't intend to make a pit stop.

I burst into the common room, then took a sharp right down the lodge's shorter leg. If I remembered correctly, Director Verity had said something about a full-size gym, which sounded too good to be true. But she hadn't been lying. I'd been too preoccupied when I'd come down here before, but now I could tell there was definitely a gym at the far end of the hall. Sasha, my fencing coach, would have *killed* to see this place.

I turned my attention to the other doors. I already knew the last one was a bathroom, but unlike most of the other rooms I'd come across, these ones weren't marked. And the first one wasn't locked, either. When I turned the knob, it opened easily, but the room on the other side was just a storage room (and it was packed with extra bunks). I'd thought the bedrooms had seemed huge. Director Verity must not have wanted to draw attention to the fact that the camp was way less popular than they'd anticipated.

Then I tried the second room, which was certainly more interesting, though that wasn't saying much. This one was stuffed with sports equipment: baseballs, volleyballs, life jackets, even a bunch of croquet sets. I tried to picture Brooklyn hitting multicolored balls through a series of white arches, but like a problematic sketch, I couldn't get the image to settle. She'd probably waste her time calculating the viscosity of each and every hit (or maybe the velocity—I'd always had a problem keeping those words straight).

When I moved on to the third door, the last one before the bathroom, I found that the knob wouldn't turn. Why lock this one but not the others? What was Director Verity trying to hide?

I still hadn't come up with an answer when a stern voice asked, "What are you doing?"

I nearly leaped out of my skin, partly because I had a rare skin condition that made me prone to chafing but mostly because the voice had scared me half to death. But it wasn't Director Verity's. It belonged to one of the math nerds, a round-faced kid clutching one half of a Little Debbie Swiss Roll pack, the same one who'd snuck a snack on our way to Cabin Epsilon. And he hadn't come alone. There were three more math nerds stretched out in a line behind him. One of them was whistling "The Imperial March."

"Not that I mind," the kid went on. "But if you're breaking and entering, we could possibly help."

I forced myself to stand up straight. At least the hall was dim enough that they couldn't see me blush. "Oh, well, I was just exploring. Since I'm only gonna be here for a day or two, I figured it wouldn't matter if I didn't take Protractors 101."

"It's Protractors 202," he said, downing the rest of his Swiss Roll. He wiped his mouth off with his sleeve. "But I guess that's fair enough."

I eyed his chocolate-stained shirt. It looked like he'd been wearing it for at least a day or three. "Exactly how long have you been here?"

"Just since yesterday," he said. "My mom had to drop me off on her way to HestonCon. But most of the other campers only got up here this morning."

I wouldn't have admitted that my mom went to a con that didn't involve the word "comic," but maybe this Swiss Roll–snarfing math nerd was more comfortable in his own skin.

That was an uncomfortable thought.

"The best part is that I had all kinds of free time to explore. The woods behind the lodge are thicker than my granddad's mustache." He looked back and forth between us, his eyes wider than full moons. "Hey, have you guys heard the legend about Old Man Archimedes?"

I perked up despite myself. "There's a legend?" I replied.

The math nerd nodded so hard the freckles that stippled his skin nearly vaulted off his face. "I've only picked up bits and pieces, but the guy who owned this land was an old dude named Archimedes." He lowered his voice. "When he died, he left the land to Director Verity, but some people say his ghost still stalks Lookout Hill at night, hooting like a restless owl while it searches for fresh meat."

A shiver skittered down my spine. I didn't believe in ghosts (whether they hooted or not), but Toby said legends were almost always based on facts.

One of the others rolled his eyes. *"Anyway,"* he said, "the counselors wanted us to tell you that it's almost time to eat."

He was the shortest of the bunch, with brown skin and a gap-toothed smile. The soccer jersey he was wearing, which was plastered with the Cuban flag, looked two or three sizes too big.

The Swiss Roll–snarfing kid took the subject change in stride. "Do you want to eat with us?"

"Well, not really *with us* with us. But you could sit at the same table."

I shook my head to clear it. If they weren't going to let some half-baked legend get to them, I couldn't let it get to me. Besides, I couldn't help but grin as I surveyed their hopeful faces. I'd spent most of May sitting with David and his friends at lunch, but that was just because I'd forced myself onto his campaign staff. These boys might have been math nerds, but at least they *wanted* me to sit with them.

I made a show of shrugging. "I guess so," I said oh-so-casually. "Even artists have to eat."

A jolt of nervous energy rippled through the pack. If I'd been trying to draw them, I would have used squiggly lines.

"So where are you guys from?" I asked as we headed toward the mess hall.

A chorus of mumbled voices answered me. I thought I caught an "Eden" and maybe even a "Kaysville," but I'd never heard of either.

"Eden sounds nice," I replied, since that would still be a true statement even if they hadn't said it. "I'm from Shepherd's Vale. It's an hour or two in that direction." I pointed left, then right. "Or maybe that direction. I'm not very good with right and left."

They just stood there blinking. Had I really been that off?

I cleared my throat and tried again. "For the record, my name's Esther—"

"We *know*," someone interrupted.

"—but you never told me yours."

No one said anything at first. Then they said everything at once.

I held up my hands. "Well, that's never gonna work, so let's come up with something else." I thought about it for a second. "How about nicknames? That's a camp thing, isn't it?"

"Nicknames?" one of them asked. "What do you mean, like Butch or Chip?"

"Well, those would be dumb nicknames, but something

like that, yes." I pointed at the whistling kid. "You could be Whistler, for instance."

"Would that be too literal?"

"Haven't you heard of *Whistler's Mother*?" When he shook his head, I sighed. "It's one of the most famous examples of nineteenth-century realism, and James Abbott McNeill Whistler was the guy who painted it." I pointed at the first kid who'd been brave enough to talk. "And you could be, say, Munch."

He'd just pulled another Swiss Roll out of his left cargo pocket, but when I called him out, he stopped and eyed it skeptically, then shrugged and ate it, anyway. "I know what you're thinking," he replied, "but I have a high metabolism." He rubbed his swollen stomach, which was as round as his face. "Or at least I will someday."

I held up my hands again. "Hey, I'm not trying to judge. I just have a thing for Edvard Munch. Well, technically, it's pronounced 'Munk,' but it looks like 'Munch' on paper." When they just stood there blinking, I felt inclined to add, "You guys have heard of *The Scream*, right? But did you know that thieves have tried to steal it, like, six or seven times?"

Munch's eyes narrowed. "I bet I'd make an awesome thief."

I couldn't guess why he'd said that—which was why I wanted to hear more—but before I could press him, the black-haired math nerd raised his hand.

"So what's my nickname?" he demanded.

I looked him up and down. His skin was darker than the soccer fan's, and now that we were standing almost on each other's toes, I could tell he was taller than I was by a handful of inches.

"Nothing comes to mind," I said, trying not to sound annoyed. I was taller than most boys and didn't like it when I wasn't. "What's your non-nickname again?"

"Marshane," he said defiantly as he stuck out his chin.

"Sounds good to me," I said, sliding my phone out of my pocket. I'd never come across a chin with such a regal-looking cleft. "Mind if I take a picture for my sketchbook?"

"Not at all," he said, like people asked him for his picture at least several times a day. "Which way would you like me to stand?"

Munch's stomach growled. "Not to interrupt," he said, "but it's almost time for dinner."

I took the photo with one hand and waved toward the mess hall with the other. "After you," I said.

The math nerds mumbled to themselves as we made our way through the common room, where the First Problem was still just sitting there, silently waiting to be solved. Other chalkboards had been scribbled on as the afternoon had dragged along, but that one had gone untouched. I wondered if they'd looked at it sideways, upside down, and backward. In painting, like in life, you had to mix up your perspective.

I didn't realize I'd stopped until the math nerds stopped beside me. They hemmed and hawed for a few seconds, and then Munch finally said, "That one's a tricky beast. We're still working it out."

I shook my head to clear it. "Oh, I know," I said. They must have thought that I'd been judging them. "And it's not a big deal. I was just thinking you could try—"

"You were thinking?" someone asked. That someone sounded like Brooklyn. "I didn't think artists knew how to use their brains."

CHAPTER 5

If Brooklyn was auditioning for the role of Mean Girl at a Summer Camp, she was doing a great job. I'd dealt with haters in the past, but she took it to the extreme. Still, the best way to deal with critics was to simply ignore them, so I pretended not to notice.

But that was the wrong thing to do.

No sooner had I tried to weave around her than she grabbed me by my sleeve. "Did you hear me?" she demanded. "Or are you also deaf?"

I glanced down at her hand, which was still attached to my right sleeve, then back up at her face. "There's nothing wrong with being deaf." I took hold of her wrist and calmly pinched a pressure point. She couldn't help but let me go. "*Or* being artistic."

I tried to walk away again, but apparently, Brooklyn wasn't finished.

"I know what you're doing," she replied, "and it's not going to work! Did you think you could just waltz in here and be the cool kid on the block? Just because they're treating you like some kind of major general doesn't mean you really are!"

The math nerds shrank away from Brooklyn, but I finally turned around. You could only take so many jabs before you had to launch your own attack.

"It's not my fault I'm *interesting*."

"Is 'interesting' your word for 'dumb'?"

Now that was a low blow. Why did everyone assume I was a moron? Math was my second-best subject, but I wasn't about to admit that. I didn't want her to think I was lying (or, worse, that she'd gotten to me).

"Are you done?" I asked.

She'd been smirking like a chimp who'd just thrown a turd at its zookeepers, but that made her scowl again. "Not quite," she said threateningly as her hands tightened into fists.

I crouched instinctively, my muscles tensed to spring. I felt exposed without my foil, so I'd have to improvise. But I hadn't come up with a plan when a door opened behind us and Director Verity appeared.

"Brooklyn, Esther!" she barked. "What in the name of Euclid are you doing?"

Brooklyn flinched, then dropped her fist. "Nothing, Director Verity."

"It didn't look like nothing." She stuck both hands on her hips. "I insist that you apologize!"

Brooklyn's nose crinkled, but Director Verity was deadly serious. Her nostrils were practically smoking.

Brooklyn blinked and mumbled, "Sorry."

She didn't sound very sincere, but I didn't call her on it. I only had to keep my head down and survive the next few hours.

Director Verity leveled a finger at Brooklyn. "If I *ever* hear you threaten one of your fellow number crunchers, I'll send you home, you understand?" When Brooklyn nodded, she sighed. "Now take your dinner to your room. You're not welcome on this floor for the remainder of the evening."

Brooklyn started to argue, then wisely changed her mind. After glaring at me one last time, she sharply spun around, grabbed a grilled cheese sandwich from the kitchen, and tromped up to her room.

As soon as she disappeared, Director Verity set her sights on Mr. Pearson (who'd drifted out of the kitchen). "Where were you while this was happening?"

Her tone should have curled his nose hairs, but Mr. Pearson only shrugged. "Making dinner," he replied.

Director Verity looked around. "And Mr. Sharp? Ms. Gutierrez?"

"We were cleaning up," the female counselor said. She and Mr. Sharp had just appeared. "We came as soon as we heard shouting."

Director Verity sighed. "All right." Then she set her sights on me. "My apologies, Esther. I'm afraid we're all on edge today." She looked me up and down. "Did she hurt you in any way?"

"I'm fine," was all I said. If I could take on Hector and Samantha, Shepherd Vale's resident bullies, I could handle one math nerd.

After Director Verity retreated to the kitchen, the rest of us followed. The others tried to cheer me up, but I was tired of pretending. I just wanted to go home.

As if in answer to my prayers, Toby rumbled down the stairs, took one look at my face, and asked, "Rough day?"

I collapsed onto the nearest bench. "That would be one way to put it."

He sat down next to me and awkwardly patted my shoulder. I scooted away as if he'd shocked me. He still looked like Toby, but maybe they'd sucked out his brains and replaced him with a shoulder-patting cyborg.

"Who painted *Guernica*?" I asked.

"Pablo Picasso," he said. "Why?"

With a heavy sigh, I scooted back. "No reason," I said glumly, plopping my chin into my hands.

He tilted his head to the side. It looked like he was

wondering if he should address my issues, but since I didn't usually have issues, he probably didn't know how to ask. "How's your room?" he asked instead.

"Pink," I said. "How's yours?"

"Fishy," he replied.

"Do you mean that literally or metaphorically?"

He shrugged. "Take your pick."

I couldn't help but snort.

"I've already tried to call your mom, but the storm's still interfering." His massive forehead wrinkled. "I hope she isn't worried."

"Oh, she's worried," I replied as I whipped out my own phone. I waved it over my head, but it couldn't find a signal. "Yeah, my phone's not working, either."

Apparently, this news didn't surprise him, because he changed the subject. "I was thinking about rescuing your duffel."

"I don't see the point," I said. "We'll be out of here by morning. My clothes will be dry by then."

He started to say something, then changed his mind at the last second. "You'll want your sketchbook, though, won't you?"

I narrowed my eyes. Toby didn't usually start something unless he meant to finish it, but then, I *did* want my sketchbook. Maybe it was best not to overanalyze.

I glanced out the window. "Is it safe to go out in the storm?"

"Safe enough," he said. "Do you want to come along?"

I didn't think, just nodded. Even if he was acting weird, I still trusted Toby more than I trusted anyone, and if I didn't get out of this lodge, there was a good chance I'd explode.

"We'll go after dinner," he replied, then got up to get his food. Mom would have hovered for a while, tried to get me to discuss my feelings, but Toby gave me room to breathe. It was one of his best qualities.

Once he was halfway through the line, I got up to get *my* food. The counselors served the grub, but since it was only grilled cheese and tomato soup, there wasn't much to serve. Ms. Gutierrez greeted me by name and asked if I was enjoying my summer as she ladled soup into my bowl, but Mr. Sharp ignored me as he gave me my sandwich. His glasses reflected my uncustomary scowl.

Director Verity overcompensated by giving me two handfuls of crackers. "I trust you've settled in?" she asked, though it sounded less like a question and more like a command: *If you haven't settled in, there are going to be consequences.*

I swallowed, hard. "Yeah, sure."

I tried to sneak away, but Director Verity cut me off.

"I'm sorry again about Brooklyn. Her father was recently transferred to the Air Force base near Layton, so I strongly suspect she's still trying to adjust." She sent me a sideways glance. "I hope the other number crunchers have made you feel more welcome?"

This sounded like a loaded question, too, and the last thing I wanted to do was get the other math nerds in trouble. "Oh, yeah, they've been great." Angeline bordered on suffocating, but I decided not to mention that. "And the digs are pretty sweet."

Director Verity looked around. The stainless steel practically sparkled. "They *are* pretty sweet, aren't they?" She gave me a third handful of crackers. "We may not be as large as Camp Vermeer, but what we lack in enrollment, we more than make up for in heart."

Of course, one of her math nerds had just tried to assault me, but I didn't point that out, just let the director have her moment. Once it had gone on long enough, I said, "Well, I should probably go. I think my soup is getting cold."

She blinked. "Oh, yes, of course."

I retrieved one of the crackers that had fallen off my tray, then headed over to the dining room. Whistler was eyeing me like I had Swiss cheese for brains, and though it looked like Munch and Marshane might have been saving me a seat, they were now arguing so loudly I didn't want to interrupt. I would have been lying if I'd said their rejections didn't sting, but before I could decide how I was going to respond, Angeline leaped to her feet.

"Hey, Esther, over here!"

Without so much as glancing at the others, I crossed the dining room and sat down next to Angeline. I expected her to launch into a recap of Math Genius, since she couldn't possibly have heard about my run-in with Brooklyn, but somehow, she had.

"Brooklyn's a piece of work," she said, crumbling crackers into her soup. "Just because you don't do math doesn't mean you *can't* do math."

"Who said I don't do math?" I asked.

Angeline grimaced. "I meant you don't do math for fun. *Everyone* does math at school. And I bet you're great at long division."

I was a pro at long division, but that had nothing to do with it. The fact of the matter was, these math nerds didn't respect me. They might have followed me around and invited me to sit with them, but in the end, Brooklyn was right. They didn't see me as an equal; they saw me as an artist.

The only way to prove them wrong was to solve the First Problem.

CHAPTER 6

Solving the First Problem without the math nerds' interference wasn't going to be easy. If they knew what I was up to, they'd probably want to help. But I couldn't impress them if I let them solve it for me. I had to solve it on my own.

I was turning in my dishes when Angeline crept up behind me and offered to show me some dance moves. Thankfully, I'd already committed to help Toby get my duffel, so I had a ready-made excuse. Except when I caught up with Toby, I told him one of the math nerds had offered to teach me how to calculate the square root of two using nothing but toothpicks.

I figured Toby would see through me, so I didn't try to sound convincing, but he didn't even arch an eyebrow. That made me feel guilty—ever since he and Mom had accidentally locked me in their ice cream parlor and I *hadn't* eaten myself sick, they'd trusted me implicitly—but it wasn't like I was about to break the law. This was practically homework.

As soon as Toby headed out, I made a beeline for the stairs. Most of the math nerds had retreated to the common room, so as long as I steered clear of Brooklyn, the second floor was mine. At the top of the stairs, I automatically turned left, then wheeled around at the last second. I'd never bothered to find out what was at the far end of the bridge that stretched across the dining room, and now seemed like a good time.

It turned out to be two bathrooms, one for girls and one for boys. I couldn't speak for the boys' bathroom, but the girls' one was much bigger than the bathroom I'd changed in. Seven sinks lined the left wall, and seven stalls lined the right one. The showers were around the corner. Everything was bone white or sage green and one-hundred-percent spotless. Either Director Verity had an army of maids at her disposal, or Camp Archimedes didn't get a lot of use.

I holed up in the third stall, which was barely lighter than a cave. After giving my poor eyes a few minutes to adjust, I perched on the edge of the toilet and pulled out the wad of napkins I'd stockpiled during dinner. Since I always had a pencil (or, more often, a paintbrush), I had something to write with. It was time to make some magic.

The first thing I did was write the problem down from memory:

You walk into a room with three sets of balanced scales.

On the first scale, two red balls and one blue ball balance with two yellow balls and a one-pound weight.

On the second scale, four red balls and a one-pound weight balance with one blue ball and one yellow ball.

On the third scale, one red ball and two yellow balls balance with one blue ball and one yellow ball.

How much does each ball weigh?

The second thing I did was chew on the end of my pencil. It was what I always did when I was working something out, and this was the most important problem I'd ever had to solve.

I was still chewing on my pencil when the bathroom door swung open and a pair of combat boots appeared. Instinctively, I tucked my feet up, sticking my arms out for balance, but if I was about to be discovered, there was nothing I could do. I didn't notice I'd stopped breathing until the combat-boot-wearing newcomer chose another stall.

If I'd paid closer attention to everyone's footwear, I would have already known which of the girls wore combat boots. Since I hadn't paid attention, I was forced to work it out while the newcomer did her business. They looked too small for an adult, and since I doubted they were Angeline's, they had to be Brooklyn's.

A lump of acid clogged my throat. If she found out I was in here—if she found out what I was doing—she'd probably tell the other math nerds. I wasn't afraid of her right hook, but I *was* afraid of failing.

I didn't want to prove her right.

The flushing of the toilet snapped me back to the moment, and I realized how bad it smelled. I had no idea how I hadn't noticed it before. I draped my arm over my nose, but that didn't really help.

As soon as the bathroom door swung shut, I launched myself out of my hiding place and bolted for the window. The rain hadn't let up, but I wrenched the window open anyway, then pressed my face against the screen. The air smelled like spring water tasted, bone-achingly cold but still refreshing. It only took a few deep breaths for my head—and nose—to clear.

I was still sucking oxygen when a lightning bolt arced across the sky. Though the sun hadn't yet set, the cloud cover made it murky, and with a not-so-distant ridgeline looming over Camp Archimedes, our corner of the mountain was already wreathed in gloom. But the lightning bolt beat back the darkness, and for a second, maybe less, I could see everything clearly: the rocks, the trees, the hill sloping up behind the lodge. And the furtive-looking figure creeping through the pouring rain.

I ducked down instinctively, digging my nails into the ledge. Goose bumps scuttled up my arms, but I scrubbed them out at once. Just because there was a ghost with the same name as the camp didn't mean I'd seen a ghost. Besides, ghosts weren't even real. It was probably just Mr. Pearson taking out the trash or something.

But if that was the case, why was he prowling around?

I counted to fifteen, then snuck a peek over the ledge. I couldn't *see* him anymore, but that didn't mean he'd disappeared. I eyed the last spot I'd seen him for another couple of minutes, then, when he didn't reappear, finally let myself relax. Unfortunately, it took my pulse a few more minutes to slow down.

Another lightning bolt arced across the stormy sky, and I noticed that the window that belonged to the locked room had been left open a crack. Adrenaline surged through my veins. I still wanted to find out what Director Verity was hiding, and there wouldn't be a better place to work on the First Problem. If I got really lucky, I could score two hits with one lunge.

I took another look around the room. It also had a sliding

door with a balcony attached. They must have wanted it to match the other windows on this wall. My heart started to pound as I returned the napkins to my pocket, then slid the screen out of the way and climbed onto the balcony.

The rain had slacked off a little, but the floor and railing were still soaked. Luckily, I hadn't put my shoes back on, so my feet were sure to stick. While I flexed my toes to warm them up, I carefully plotted my descent. Whatever moron had designed this lodge had cleared away the trees in the immediate vicinity, so there was no way to climb down, but a foot-wide ledge ran the full length of the lodge and wrapped around the inside corner. It was probably supposed to be decorative, but it might as well have been a sidewalk for my tricky feet (though Sasha would have called it "my spectacular footwork").

After drawing a deep breath, I climbed over the railing and slid onto the ledge. It actually ran into the balcony, so I didn't even have to stretch. The ledge was slipperier than I'd expected, but I didn't let that stop me, just curled my toes around the edge and pressed my back into the wall.

I'd nearly reached the inside corner when another lightning bolt bathed the landscape in pure white. It was so beautiful I couldn't help but stop to stare—until a raindrop landed in my eye and the thunder nearly knocked me flat. After regaining my balance, I bypassed the first two windows, but halfway between the second and the third, my foot slipped out from under me and I went down, hard. My hip hit the ledge first, but my momentum rolled me over. As I scrabbled for a handhold, it was all that I could do not to tumble off the ledge.

I bit my lip to keep from crying out. My hip was going to be black-and-blue, and I'd probably lost a few more toenails, but this was no time to freak out. Brooklyn's digestive system might have been distracting her, but I figured she would hear me if I cut loose and screamed.

Since I was already dangling from the ledge, I decided to let go and take my chances with the drop. It was longer than I'd thought, so when I finally hit the ground (or something closer to the ground), I couldn't help but lose my balance. At least the bushes broke my fall.

After picking myself up and brushing off the leaves and muck, I stumbled over to the window. For a second, I worried that I'd imagined the whole thing, but the window was still open (and it didn't even have a screen). I pushed it open wide enough to admit one cold, wet girl, then threw one leg over the windowsill and boosted myself up.

It was darker than I'd expected, but my feet still found the puddle pooling under the window. As silently as an assassin, I pushed the window closed and waited for my eyes to adjust. Director Verity might have fooled the math nerds, but she couldn't fool me.

But when the lightning flashed again, it was plain to see

that it was just another storage room. Cardboard boxes lined one wall, and plastic buckets lined another. There was even an old easel in the corner, like a kid sent to time-out. Had they stolen it from Camp Vermeer?

After wringing out my soggy shirt—Angeline's shirt, actually—and shoving my curls out of my face, I hunkered down next to the puddle and pulled out my napkins. They were slightly waterlogged, but I'd put napkins through worse. After finding a (mostly) dry one, I pulled out my pencil and went back to work.

I read back through the problem, but it made no more sense down here than it had up in the bathroom. I didn't even notice I was doodling until I'd drawn a very official-looking scale, with heavy plates and ropelike chains. On a whim, I added two red balls—which I labeled with two Rs—and a blue ball to one side, then two yellow balls and a one-pound weight to the other. Then I drew another scale with four red balls and a one-pound weight on one side and two more balls, one blue and one yellow, on the other.

My heart started to thump as I sketched the third and final scale. This wasn't a math problem; it was an art one. And I happened to be Camp Archimedes's resident artist.

While I stared at the scales, waiting for lightning to strike, I doodled balls and weights around the edges of the page. I tried to decide how many blues were the same as one yellow or how many yellows were the same as a single red, but I just kept seeing circles. On another whim, I redrew the scales with other shapes instead of balls—and immediately noticed that the right side of the second scale was the same as the right side of the third.

I scribbled a new scale with four reds and a one-pounder on one side and one red and two yellows on the other, balancing the *left* side of the second scale with the *left* side of the third. It took me a few tries and all but one of my napkins, but I solved it. I *solved* it.

The math nerds were going to flip.

I was lying on my back when I woke up the next morning. Normally, my ceiling, which Toby and I had painted to look like the cosmos, greeted me when I woke up, so the bottom of a bunk was a major disappointment. I was tempted to roll over and try to go back to sleep—until I remembered that I'd solved it. The First Freaking Problem.

I sat straight up in bed, banging my head on the top bunk. I kept the groaning to a minimum, but Brooklyn still rolled over.

"Could you be any louder?"

A part of me wanted to throw one of my dirty socks at her (and after a day of tromping through the mud, they were bound to be especially dirty), but I forced myself to resist. The fact that my dirty socks were stuffed in my shoes downstairs might have had something to do with it. "Sorry," I said instead.

Angeline stretched like a cat. Did she practice stretching, or were some girls just born that way? "What time is it?" she asked.

My fingers scrabbled for my phone until I remembered that I'd left it in the pocket of the pants Angeline had let me borrow. "I don't know," I said as I glanced out the window. I'd once spent a whole summer doing studies of sunrises, so I should have been an expert on figuring out what time it was based on the position of the sun. I *should* have been, but I wasn't. "Seven thirty, maybe?"

"Seven thirty?" she replied as she tumbled out of bed. "We're going to miss times table sprints!"

I couldn't have cared less about times table sprints, since I was planning to be gone by lunchtime at the latest. And since I'd already conquered the unconquerable First Problem.

While Angeline threw on a fresh shirt and *another* pair of sparkly pants, I retrieved the shirt she'd let me borrow— which was now splattered with dried mud—and lobbed it at Brooklyn's head. "Up and at 'em, sunshine! Don't want to miss times table sprints."

The muddy shirt missed her by a mile, so she didn't even stir. "Times table sprints are for third graders."

"Oh, come on," I said. "Times table sprints can't be *that* bad."

"You're right," she said. "They're worse."

These darts were aimed at Angeline, but she didn't let them pierce her, just folded her arms across her waist. "You might as well get up. You know Director Verity won't let you skip."

"Yeah," Brooklyn replied, finally climbing out of bed, "because I'm not director's pet."

This insult made me flinch, but if it bothered Angeline, it didn't bother her for long.

"Are you ready?" she asked me, thoroughly ignoring Brooklyn.

I glanced over at Brooklyn, who was switching out one dingy sports bra for another, then at Angeline, who was pretending not to care that we were going to be late. I wanted to be there for Angeline (especially since she'd been there for me), but I also wanted to make sure that Brooklyn didn't try to dawdle. I needed her in that common room when I solved the First Problem.

"Almost," I replied as I pretended to rummage through my duffel for a can of body spray. The bag had been waiting for me when I slunk back in last night, evidence of Toby's awesomeness. "I just need to freshen up . . ."

I didn't know how to end that sentence, but Angeline

didn't seem to care. She did this awkward arm-wave thing—it must have been a hip-hop move—and practically skipped out the door. It banged shut on her heels with a satisfying *smack*.

As soon as Angeline was gone, Brooklyn kicked the muddy shirt at me. "You can cut the crap," she said. "I know you don't use that smelly stuff any more than I do."

"Maybe," I admitted, hugging my sketchbook for support. "But if you think for one second that that makes you and me the same, you can stop thinking that right now."

Brooklyn didn't bother to reply, just stuffed her feet into her combat boots and stalked out of the room. I was still trying to decide if I felt more grateful or insulted as I hurried after her.

I'd just crossed the second bridge when I found myself surrounded by a cluster of math nerds. Munch was in the lead, but the rest weren't far behind. They were so busy arguing about irrational numbers that they barely noticed me. I didn't bother to cut in as we tumbled down the stairs and spilled into the mess hall.

Director Verity was manning the first station. "Good morning, Esther!" she said brightly, dumping a scoop of egg balls on my plate. Mom said that scrambled eggs were surprisingly tricky, but I would have thought that someone with a math degree could have figured them out. "I trust you got a good night's sleep?"

"More or less," I said as I took two strips of bacon from

a silent Mr. Sharp. These looked slightly more edible, but only because he'd burned them to a crisp.

"Excellent, just excellent," Director Verity replied. "We've got lots of activities lined up, so you're going to need to get your rest. We certainly want to make the most of the time you have to spend with us!"

I couldn't contain a sneaky grin. "Oh, I'm planning to," I said. Last night's scribbled-on napkins were nestled safely in my pocket.

I nudged my tray along, accepting pancakes from Mr. Pearson and fresh fruit from Ms. Gutierrez, but at the drinks station, I stopped. Toby was pouring orange juice while decked out in a bright red apron that said KISS THE COOK.

"How'd they rope you into this?" I asked.

Toby's shoulders rose and fell. "I already ate," he said.

"You always were a softy," I replied, taking a picture of him for good measure. Mom was going to find that apron all kinds of hilarious. "Speaking of which, thanks for dropping off my duffel. It's nice to have my sketchbook back." I checked both ways for Angeline, then cupped a hand around my mouth. "And it's even nicer to be back in my own clothes."

Toby's beard twitched slightly. "I thought the sparkles suited you."

I socked him in the shoulder, but he didn't sock me back. He never bothered to react. It was kind of irritating.

"I checked the weather report," he said. "It's supposed to rain today."

I felt my shoulders fall. "We were supposed to *leave* today."

Toby cleared his throat. "About that," he replied, sending me a sideways glance. "Are you sure you want to go?"

"Of course I'm sure!" I said, then remembered the napkin in my pocket. But Toby couldn't know that I'd solved the First Problem. "Why wouldn't I be?"

"I don't know," he said, but from the way that he was bouncing, it was clear he really did. "I guess it just seemed like this place was growing on you."

"Growing on me," I replied. "What do you mean, like diaper rash?"

"Don't insult them," Toby said. "You should know better than most that we're all artists in our own way."

I lowered my gaze. I hated it when Toby made me feel bad (though it was usually because I deserved it).

Toby cleared his throat. "Anyway, the truck's not in great shape, so it can't stay where it is." He motioned toward Mr. Sharp, who was still dispensing bacon. "Gordon said he'd help me tow it. We're gonna head down after breakfast."

"Won't that be dangerous?" I asked.

"No more dangerous than welding rebar, and I've done that plenty of times." He sent me a sideways glance. "You could come with us, if you want. We could always use a lookout."

"Thanks for the offer," I replied. "There's something I need to do first, but if I've wrapped it up by then, I'll definitely go with you."

Toby dipped his head, then poured another glass of orange juice. I sat down next to Marshane, since Angeline was nowhere to be found. She must have eaten fast.

I tried to tune the math nerds out, but that was easier said than done. Munch and the soccer fan couldn't come to an agreement on who would win in a street fight, Star-Lord or Gamora. They kept trying to get me to take sides, but even though I had a strong opinion (Gamora, no question, since Star-Lord's attention span was no longer than his pinkie and fights were all about staying focused under pressure), I didn't let them draw me in. The napkins in my pocket suddenly felt as heavy as a bag of bricks. I'd always liked being the center of attention, but the thought of talking math in front of a quotient of math nerds was enough to make me sick. What if I'd gotten it wrong? What if I really was a stupid artist?

I was so busy freaking out that I almost missed the moment when Director Verity cleared her throat. "Good morning, number crunchers!"

The others parroted, "Good morning," but with less enthusiasm.

"And now for our first order of business," Director Verity went on. "Has anyone solved the First Problem?"

She surveyed the dining room through narrowed eyes. I

honestly couldn't tell whether she wanted us to say yes or no, but whether she wanted it or not, I was about to lay it on her.

Slowly, very slowly, I raised my hand. "I have."

CHAPTER 7

An awkward hush fell over the dining room, and I lowered my hand. Director Verity hadn't called on me, but it seemed dumb to leave it up there.

Finally, she cleared her throat. "That's excellent, Esther." Apparently, "excellent" was her word of the day. She produced a piece of chalk from nowhere. "Would you care to put it on the board?"

I gulped. I'd worked in chalk before, but never on a real, live chalkboard. Still, I couldn't *not* put my solution on the board, so I slid out of my seat, took the chalk out of her hands, and slunk into the next room. The math nerds followed me as I marched up to that chalkboard with as much confidence as I could muster. The chalk felt cool in my hand, but it also felt familiar, like a long-lost friend who'd just come in from the cold.

"It's just a picture," I explained as I drew three scales on the board. "One scale has two reds and a blue on one side and two yellows and a one-pounder on the other. Another has four reds and a one-pounder on one side and a blue and a yellow on the other. And the last scale has a red and two yellows on one side and a blue and a yellow on the other."

It would have been nice if I'd had my pastels so I could color-code the balls, but the only thing I had was this one piece of off-white chalk. Still, I put it to good use. I drew circles for the red balls, squares for the yellow, triangles for the blue, and stars for the one-pound weights.

"I thought they were balls," Marshane piped up. I should have known he'd be the heckler.

"They *are* balls," I replied. "You can think of the different shapes as symbols." I motioned toward the mumbo jumbo they'd written on the other boards. "You guys like symbols, right?"

At least that shut him up.

I drew a fortifying breath. "The first thing you have to notice—or at least the first thing *I* noticed—is that one side of the second scale and one side of the third scale are the same. So that means four reds and a one-pounder must balance with one red and two yellows." I drew another scale to represent it. "Does that make sense so far?"

The math nerds didn't answer, but Director Verity smiled. I figured that meant I was headed in the right direction.

"Now there are reds on both sides of the scale, so we can take one off both sides"—I erased two of the circles—"so now we have three reds and a one-pounder balancing with two yellows. So if we add one-pounders to both sides of *this* scale"—I added two stars to my drawing—"we'll have three reds and two one-pounders balancing with two yellows and a one-pounder, which is what we have on the right side of the first scale."

I stopped to double-check my work. The math nerds were leaning in, like they were paying close attention, and Director Verity had gone from smiling to squinting and taking notes. I couldn't decide if that was good or bad, but since she hadn't cut me off, I decided to keep going.

"In other words," I said as I drew another scale, "three reds and two one-pounders are the same as two reds and one blue." I erased two red balls on both sides. "That means that one red and two one-pounders are the same as one blue. So if we substitute one red and two one-pounders for the one blue on the second scale"—I quickly made this switch—"then we have four reds and a one-pounder balancing with one red, one yellow, and two one-pounders." I erased the extra symbols. "And *that's* the same as three reds balancing with a yellow and a one-pounder."

I stepped back to survey my work—and to give Director Verity and the math nerds a little time to breathe. If they held their breath much longer, they were probably going to faint. I'd better wrap this up, and fast.

"At first, I couldn't figure out how to get rid of that extra one-pound weight, but then it occurred to me that, if a red ball *was* one pound, it would be easy to subtract them." I erased the one-pound weight on one side and a red ball on the other. "And when I made that substitution, all the other scales still balanced." I found the last blank spot of chalkboard and scribbled down the answer. "Red is one pound, yellow's two, and blue is—you guessed it—three."

My voice squeaked on the last words, but I couldn't help myself. I was as nervous as a turkey on the day before Thanksgiving. After dusting off my hands, I waited for someone to swoop in and say I'd messed up the addition and gotten the whole problem wrong. But the math nerds didn't budge. Brooklyn's glare had morphed into a stare, and Whistler was no longer whistling. I was tempted to run off and take my chances with the gully, but before I could get my feet to respond, Director Verity lassoed me. Her nails dug into my shoulder.

"Esther Lambert," she said slowly, like she was sampling my name, deciding if it was sweet or salty. "Not only did you solve the First Problem"—her face split into a wide grin—"but your solution strategy is one I've never seen before!"

I didn't have a chance to fully process what she'd said before Marshane whistled and the rest of the common room exploded with applause. It wasn't like I'd won the seventh-grade election, but it still felt like the world—or at least Camp Archimedes—was in the palm of my hand.

Once the applause died down, Director Verity clicked her heels. "Now that Esther has solved the First Problem, let's continue on with the day's activities." She gave my shoulder one last squeeze. "I know times table sprints might feel beneath you, but I've found that memory drills are the best way to calm the mind."

"I like times table sprints," I lied, since I suddenly felt like a math nerd.

Her grin exposed both rows of teeth. "I'm sure you do," was all she said.

I'd never been a gloater, but I was proud of that solution. There really was something to be said for thinking outside the box and looking at a problem from a completely different angle. After taking a sly shot of my solution on the board, I tried to get in touch with Mom so I could tell her the good news, but my phone still had no bars. I guess that explained why the director hadn't taken them away from us—she must have known they wouldn't work.

News of my solution spread like wildfire—which was to

say it only took an hour for the three people who hadn't heard it to come up and congratulate me. Mr. Sharp, who'd stepped into the bathroom during my three minutes of fame, actually said, "Nice job," and Graham, who'd been late to breakfast, awkwardly patted my back. But it was Angeline's reaction that took me by surprise.

"You solved the First Problem?" Her eyes were as round as harvest moons. "You *solved* the First *Problem?*"

I felt my cheeks get hot, but it must have been because we were now sitting by the fireplace. We were supposed to be weaving dream catchers with Fibonacci spirals, but even though they'd shown me tons of photos (including a dozen of a snail from every imaginable angle), I couldn't tell the difference between a Fibonacci spiral and every other kind of spiral. Luckily, I'd made multiple dream catchers before, so my weaving was spot-on. But Angeline couldn't have cared less.

"Well, yeah," I said uncomfortably. "Is that really so surprising?"

She lowered her gaze. "I didn't mean it like that, Esther. I just meant that you *solved* it—and in near-record time, too."

I scratched the back of my head. "Well, no one had done it yet, but we've only been here for a day."

"Oh, right," Angeline replied. "It's not like *I've* seen someone solve it. It's just that there's a list in Director Verity's office. The current record is three hours, but only a few people have solved it in less than twenty-four." Before I could ask what she'd been doing in Director Verity's office, Angeline held up her dream catcher. "So what do you think?"

She was clearly trying to change the subject, but I didn't mind. When it came to congratulations, I preferred the silent treatment. It was better when people underestimated you. Then they couldn't see you coming.

"I think it's great," I said. Not only did her dream catcher look exactly like a snail, but her weaving was neat and even. "You should start stringing your feathers."

Angeline didn't reply, just kept making eyes at Graham. He was clearly concentrating, because his tongue was sticking out. It might have been cute if it hadn't been disgusting.

"Angeline," I said, waving a hand in front of her face. When she didn't respond, I added, "Look, I know he's kind of cute when he's not sticking his tongue out, but we're supposed to be working."

Angeline shook her head. "Wait, what?" she asked, blinking. Then she followed my line of sight. "Oh, *Graham.* Yeah, he's adorable." Her pixie nose crinkled. "But he's also obtuse."

I had no idea what "obtuse" meant, but I didn't take the time to ask. If she was trying to distract me, she was totally failing. I knew smitten when I saw it.

When Graham scrambled to his feet, Angeline scrambled to hers. "I've got to split," she said.

"Where are you going?" I demanded.

"Private tutoring," she said. "I'm trying to skip Algebra 1."

I seriously doubted that—she was probably in Algebra 2—but she was welcome to her secrets. "Oh, okay. That's cool."

She flung her dream catcher in my face. "Would you turn it in for me? I'd turn it in myself . . ."

"But you're supposed to meet Director Verity." I took her nearly flawless dream catcher. "Yeah, sure, I'll turn it in."

Instead of handing it to me, she let it tumble to the ground, then quietly crept after Graham. I tried not to be offended. If she wanted to lock lips with the cutest boy in a hundred miles, that was none of my business.

Once Angeline was gone, I set my sights on the math nerds. The soccer fan's dream catcher had turned into a tangled mess that looked more like a reindeer than a Fibonacci spiral, so he was dancing it on Whistler's head, singing "Wyatt Got Run Over by a Reindeer," while Marshane tried not to snort. Another math nerd was doodling Greek letters on the back of an old worksheet, and Munch was sneaking handfuls of Chex Mix when he thought no one was looking.

I was on the verge of poking my own eye out with my needle when Mr. Pearson interrupted. It was time to eat again. At least they didn't try to starve us. But I'd only taken a few bites of pulled pork when someone tapped me on the shoulder.

"Are you ready?" Toby asked, slinging a rope over his shoulder.

I glanced around the dining room. Angeline still hadn't come back from wherever she'd run off to, and now Whistler, Marshane, and some math nerd I didn't know were smack-dab in the middle of a prime-number burping contest. Marshane had gotten up to a hundred and thirty-seven, but now they were trying to decide if a hundred and thirty-seven was prime.

I arched an eyebrow. "I've been ready since we got here." As much as I enjoyed a good prime-number burping contest, some things were more important.

Toby headed for the door. He didn't wait for me to follow, just trusted that I would, and I didn't disappoint. I'd been following him around since he and Mom had started dating when I was in the second grade. He might not have been my real dad, but you could have fooled me.

Mr. Sharp met us in the common room with two pairs of galoshes and a couple of heavy-duty ponchos. He didn't try to make small talk as we climbed into our gear, which meant that he and Toby were going to get along just fine.

When Mr. Sharp opened the door, a blast of cold air greeted us, instantly fogging up his glasses. That was summertime in the Rocky Mountains for you. Still, the rain wasn't as bad as it had been on the drive up or even during last night's explorations. My galoshes squelched agreeably as we crossed the muddy driveway and climbed into the camp's enormous truck, a bright red monstrosity with CAMP ARCHIMEDES emblazoned on both sides.

The drive down to Toby's truck took a heck of a lot less time than the hike up to the camp, and Mr. Sharp was only going ten or twelve miles an hour. When the gully appeared around a bend, Mr. Sharp flipped a careful U-turn, then slowly backed up to the bank. Once he was as close as he could get without sinking the monstrosity, he shifted into park and silently climbed out of the truck.

We used the same logs that Toby and I had used before to make our way across the gully, so by the time we reached our truck, my legs were sore and wobbly, and a thin line of sweat was dripping down the middle of my back. Toby said that exercise was nature's (mostly) foolproof way of getting your creative juices flowing, so I tried to let them flow. While they went to work with Toby's rope, I dipped my fingers in the mud the truck's tires had stirred up and added fresh smears to the boulder. It was no cave painting, but it felt good to create, to use my fingers again.

While they went back and forth between the truck and the monstrosity, I smeared more mud on the boulder. I started with geometric shapes, mostly triangles and rectangles, but it didn't take long for a larger image to emerge. I was just about to add a roof to my abstract painting of the lodge when, out of the corner of my eye, I noticed something flutter.

At first, I thought it was a leaf, but when I looked at it, *really* looked at it, I realized it was a piece of paper. Somehow, someone had tacked it to the base of the nearest tree. It could have been out here for days, except it was as white as a baby's first tooth—and nothing that insubstantial would have survived yesterday's storm.

I was tempted to ignore it, but whoever had tacked it to that tree must have known that whoever came along wouldn't be able to resist. After making sure that Toby was still busy with the truck, I waded through the rain-soaked grass and ripped the piece of paper off its nail. It was a white sheet, folded once, but on the inside were typewritten words:

```
Once upon a time, there was a camp, and
in that camp, there was a sphinx. The
sphinx's name was Sphinx, since that's
how these stories work, but since Sphinx
was the only sphinx, no one ever got
confused.

Sphinx ruled the camp, but the other mon-
sters didn't seem to notice. As far as
monsters    went,    they    were    kind    of
```

unobservant. Centaur and Unicorn kept their eyes trained on the ground as they galloped here and there, and Griffin and Pegasus had their heads stuck in the clouds. Manticore and Minotaur kept getting into fights, and Harpy and Siren only listened to themselves. Hydra had too many eyes. Cyclops didn't have enough. Phoenix might have paid attention, but Phoenix had this pesky habit of sometimes bursting into flames. Gorgon and Chimera didn't care, and frankly, Satyr was a moron.

Instead of waiting for the others to recognize its contributions, Sphinx decided to just show them. Sphinx invited them to tea, but when they arrived at Sphinx's table, Sphinx was nowhere to be found. A typewritten note was there instead:

Find the clues, then solve the puzzle.

This note made as much sense to the monsters as this story makes to you, so they paid no attention to it. The tea hadn't stopped steaming, and the sugar cubes were glistening, so they sat down at the table and spread their napkins in their laps. Pegasus had just poured the tea when Sphinx leaped out of the bushes, spotted the easiest target, and snapped Pegasus in half. The others were rightly horrified, but Sphinx didn't seem to notice, just sat down and drank the tea. Sphinxes always took a life when their riddles went unsolved. That was just what sphinxes did.

Do not make the same mistake.

I snuck peeks in both directions. I kept waiting for someone to jump out and yell, "You should have seen your face!" but the bushes barely stirred. It was like the wind itself was somehow holding its breath.

I read the note again, but it still didn't make sense. I knew what centaurs were, but I'd never heard of manticores. And what in the world was a chimera, anyway? I was about to trash the note when I remembered that centaurs had something to do with Greek mythology—and that Archimedes was an ancient Greek name.

"Hey, Esther," Toby said, startling me out of my thoughts. "We could use a little help."

"Yeah, sure," I mumbled numbly, crumpling the note into a ball. I hadn't wanted to keep thinking about Greek monsters, anyway.

"Could you grab that clamp?" he asked without bothering to point. He knew I'd know which one.

Obediently, I retrieved the clamp and handed it to Toby, but my mind was on the note, turning it over in my head like the rocks in my old tumbler. But it wasn't getting any smoother. There couldn't *really* be a killer at Camp Archimedes—right?

CHAPTER 8

The note stayed in my pocket for the rest of the afternoon. A part of me wished we could go, wished I could pretend I'd never seen it, but the truck still wasn't fixed.

And how could I ignore the note?

I kept sneaking it out and going over it again, but it made no more sense on the ninth read than it had on the first. If it was real, then it was evidence, so by not turning it over—to the police or the director—I was helping someone kill. But if it *wasn't* real (and my logical side had to admit that this was probably more likely), then screaming bloody murder would undo all the progress that I'd made. I'd go back to being the head-in-the-clouds artist. No one at Camp Archimedes would ever take me seriously again.

I was still weighing my options when Graham plopped down beside me, bouncing the beanbag I was sitting on. Since it was still drizzling outside, we were stuck in the sitting room, where Mr. Pearson was trying to teach us how to carve stuff out of wood. The goal was to make a woodcut with a shape that would tessellate (which was a fancy way of saying it could cover a flat surface with no gaps or overlaps if you stamped it a bunch of times). I was trying to keep it simple, but mine looked less like a triangle and more like a lopsided acorn.

"Looks like you could use some help," Graham said.

I surveyed my handiwork. "Yeah, I guess I could." The note sat on my thigh, as big and itchy as a boil. "I'm not really thinking straight."

He sent me a sideways glance. "That isn't what I heard."

He was obviously referring to the First Problem.

"Oh, please," I said, making a face. "You didn't even hear my answer. And if one more person asks me for a selfie, I might have to clobber him."

Graham held up his hands. "I promise not to ask you for a selfie." With a shy grin, he added, "But I'd take one if you offered."

Anxiety curled in my stomach like pencil shavings in a sharpener. Was Graham flirting with me? It certainly seemed like he was flirting. But I thought that he liked Angeline—or maybe Angeline just liked him? It was hard to keep things straight. Either way, I wasn't going to risk a friendship by flirting with some *boy*.

"Sorry," I said blithely, "but my phone is on the fritz." I craned my neck to see what he'd been working on. "So how's your woodcut coming?"

It was the same trick that Angeline had used on me, but if Graham noticed the shift, he didn't take the time to point it out. "It's a falcon," he said proudly.

And it was. Not only did his woodcut look exactly like a bird in flight, but I suspected it would tessellate as well as the rectangle we'd started with.

"You should start stamping it," I said as I nudged the paint toward him.

Reluctantly, he picked up his paper (which had slid off the beanbag and gotten stuck to his sneaker). "Yeah, I guess I should." But instead of reaching for the paint, he squinted at the other side.

My stomach did a somersault. Somehow, I knew what he was squinting at.

Graham held the paper out to me. "What is *that* supposed to mean?"

Unlike the other sheets of paper Mr. Pearson had passed out, this one was thin and smooth, and the message's type-written letters matched the letters on my note:

```
Satyr and Minotaur share a cabin with two
other monsters.
```

I snatched the clue out of his hands. "Where did you get this?" I demanded.

"From Mr. Pearson," he replied. "I took the next one in the stack."

So had the clue been meant for me and Graham had gotten in the way, or had the note been meant for Graham and I'd gotten in his way? Or were we supposed to work together? I was getting paranoid.

I must have been giving Graham the stink eye, because he leaned away from me. "Are you all right?" he asked. "I don't mean to be rude, but you're kind of scaring me."

"It's nothing," I replied. I started to give him the paper, then changed my mind at the last second. "Do you mind if I hang on to this?"

"You want to hang on to my paper?"

The way he said it made it sound like I'd just asked for his number. "*No*," I said emphatically. "I just want to keep this clue."

"Sure, you can hang on to it." But instead of backing off, he yanked the clue out of my hands. "*If* you tell me what you're up to."

I forced myself not to shudder. "What makes you think I'm up to something?"

He motioned toward the other math nerds. "You might be able to fool them, but you can't fool me," he said.

I seriously doubted that, but when I tried to fake him out

and yank the clue out of *his* hands, he easily hopped off the beanbag. I hit the floorboards with a *thud*.

Mr. Pearson jumped. "What are you doing over there?"

"Nothing, Mr. Pearson!" Graham and I replied in unison.

Mr. Pearson huffed. "Well, do *something*," he mumbled. "If you two get me in trouble, I'm going to get you in trouble, too."

He didn't wait for us to answer, just went back to his woodcut (which was slowly turning into a coyote howling at the moon). I scowled up at Graham as I dusted myself off, but he didn't seem fazed.

"Well?" he finally whispered when I didn't say anything. "Are you going to tell me or not?"

I almost told him to take a hike, then bit my tongue at the last second. What if he took it literally and got himself lost in the woods? "Meet me upstairs at nine thirty. And *don't* forget to bring that clue!"

I spent the rest of the day trying not to think about the clue, which, of course, meant that the clue was the only thing I thought about. To keep myself from going crazy, I retreated to the game room and pulled out my trusty sketchbook. Transforming my photos into sketches would (hopefully) help me calm down.

I pulled up my first photo, a panorama of the mess hall,

in my awesome drawing app, which could superimpose grids over the pictures in my phone. Then I used a borrowed ruler to draw a corresponding grid on the next page in my sketchbook. I could almost feel my bones relaxing as I measured out the lines. I would never understand why everyone wasn't an artist.

I was so focused on my sketch that I didn't hear the footsteps creeping up behind my beanbag until someone blurted, "What's that, what's that, what's that?"

My pencil lurched across the page. I looked over my shoulder, but it was just the soccer fan (whose name, I'd learned, was Federico).

"It's a drawing," I replied, unable to keep a silly grin from spreading across my face. It was hard not to be infected by his boundless energy.

He scrunched up his nose. "What's the purpose of the grid?"

I turned my phone toward him. "The photo is this big, but my sketchbook is *this* big. The grid helps me blow it up without losing the proportions."

He tapped his lips thoughtfully. "Seems like cheating," he replied.

I tried not to take offense. He was a math nerd, after all. "It's harder than it looks," I said.

He considered that, then shrugged. "I guess that's probably true." And with that, he wandered off.

I waited for him to disappear, then set my sights back on my sketch. At first, my lines were sharp and thick—I guess Federico's criticism hadn't quite rolled off my back—but as I forced myself to draw, to let the lines work themselves out, I finally got my mojo back. I was so preoccupied with texturing the fireplace that I didn't check the time for the next hour and a half. By then, it was 9:17; I'd almost missed the rendezvous.

Growling, I snapped my sketchbook shut and headed up to Cabin Epsilon for some last-minute supplies. We were going to need something to write on, so I stuffed my sketchbook down my shirt, then slid a flashlight into my pocket. I was in the middle of bundling my hair into a beanie when a cool voice said, "If I didn't know better, I'd think you were sneaking out."

I ripped the beanie off and whirled around. Angeline was standing in the doorway with both hands stuck on her hips. I started to answer, then immediately thought better of it. If I told her where I was going, she'd probably insist on going with me, and this seemed like the sort of thing to involve as few people in as possible. But if I *didn't* tell her—and if she found out I'd met Graham—what was she going to think?

"I know this looks bad," I said, backpedaling, "but it isn't what you think it is."

"What do I think it is?" she asked.

How was I supposed to answer *that*? She might as well have given me a shovel, because I kept digging myself deeper.

Angeline stuck out her chin. "Fine, don't tell me," she replied. "But when you end up in the infirmary, don't say I didn't warn you."

She tossed her hair over her shoulder, then spun around and stalked away. As her footsteps pounded down the hall, I considered going after her for about two and a half seconds. She only thought she wanted to come. If she'd known what was going on, she would have run the other way.

When I could no longer hear her footsteps, I returned my beanie to my head and slid the door open a crack. Luckily, the coast was clear, so after adjusting my sketchbook (which was part valuable tool, part security blanket), I headed down the hall behind her.

When I got to the boys' rooms, I stopped long enough to check the time. According to my phone, it was 9:30 on the nose, but Graham was still nowhere in sight. I pressed my lips into a line and stuffed my phone back in my pocket. Leave it to a math nerd not to take a death threat seriously.

I was still fuming to myself when Cabin Gamma's door jerked open and a pair of chalk-white hands dragged me into the room. I instantly dropped into a squat, grasping for a foil that wasn't there, but it was only Graham—not to mention Munch, Marshane, and the boy with the pierced ears.

"What are you *doing*?" I demanded, then motioned toward the other math nerds. "And what are they doing here?"

At least Graham had the decency to blush. "Sorry about the snatch-and-grab," he said. "We've been monitoring the hall, and it sounds like someone just went by. We didn't want them to catch us."

"That still doesn't explain what *they're* doing here," I hissed.

Marshane grinned. "Oh, that's easy," he replied, folding his arms across his chest. "You're not the only one who found a clue."

I stiffened. "Where'd you find it?"

The boy with the pierced ears, who was still guarding the door, glared at me over his shoulder. "Do you really want to talk about it here?"

I swallowed, hard. "You're right." One of the counselors could come along and hear my voice at any moment. "All right, then, let's get going."

"And where are we going?" he asked.

"To the girls' bathroom," I replied.

The boy with the pierced ears stopped.

"We can't go in *there*," Graham said.

"Sure we can," Marshane replied. "We just stick our arms out and push."

Graham's nostrils shriveled into slits. "That's not what I meant, and you know it."

"You two sound like old hens," I said. "What are you, brothers or something?"

I'd meant it as a joke, but that wasn't how Graham took it.

"We're *not* brothers," he replied. "But we go to the same school, so we . . . bump into one another."

I sent Munch a sideways glance. "Do you guys know each other, too?"

The boy with the pierced ears shook his head at the same time Munch replied, "I don't know any of these guys—or any of the girls, either."

At least that settled that. I flicked my thumb over my shoulder. "Well, are you coming or not?" When they didn't respond, I couldn't help but roll my eyes. "It's not like the girls' bathroom is the final destination. Even I'm not dumb enough to hold a super-secret meeting in a room that Brooklyn uses."

Graham stuck both hands on his hips. "What *is* the final destination?"

I couldn't help but smile smugly. "It's right out there," I said, pointing at their sliding door.

Skeptically, they huddled around it and squinted into the darkness. Though the rain had (finally) stopped, the glass was streaked with water stains, so it was hard to tell what you were looking at. But when I pointed out the storage room—and its still-open window—they drew a collective breath.

"It's the most secret place around," I said. "No one ever goes down there, and the door's locked from the inside. *But* there's a handy-dandy ledge between the girls' bathroom and that storage room. It's like walking on a sidewalk."

The boy with the pierced ears made a face. "A sidewalk twelve feet in the air."

I clapped him on the back. "Hey, no one said you had to come."

Graham shoved open the sliding door. "Forget the girls' bathroom." He hopped out onto the balcony. "We can catch the ledge from here."

"But won't we have to sneak past Director Verity's room?" the boy with the pierced ears asked.

Graham motioned toward the door. "Well, then, go ahead and sneak into the girls' bathroom, Oliver."

At least that sealed the deal. One by one, the math nerds tiptoed out onto the balcony. Maybe there was something to be said for peer pressure after all.

"Do exactly as I do," I said as I climbed over the railing. "And don't get too spread out. But don't clump so close together you take the rest of us down with you if you start to slip."

Shudders rippled through their shoulders, but they didn't try to bail. I had to give them props for that. After wiping off my hands, I transferred over to the ledge and inched my way along the wall, giving the math nerds ample room to make the transfer behind me. They climbed over the railing using a variety of techniques, Graham and Munch by straddling it, Oliver by squeezing through the widest part, and Marshane by vaulting over it as nimbly as a cat.

"Show-off," I muttered through clenched teeth, returning my attention to the ledge. The stretch between the balconies wasn't hard to navigate, but when I got to the next balcony, I raised a hand to halt the others. Candlelight was dancing out onto the balcony, spotlighting the silhouette of either Ms. Gutierrez or Director Verity. At least the blinds were closed, but if we crossed her balcony, she might be able to hear us.

I was still working out this problem when Graham tapped me on the shoulder. He pointed at the storage room, then pointed at the ground and mouthed, *Climb down here instead?*

I opened my mouth to answer, then snapped it shut again. I could think of several reasons not to climb down at this spot, but most of them amounted to, *Because it wasn't my idea.* Grudgingly, I mouthed back, *Fine,* then got down on my hands and knees and lowered myself over the edge.

This time, I landed in one of the flower beds, which was less muddy but more painful, since they were lined with chunks of tree bark. After dusting off the larger bits, I glanced up at the ledge to see how the others were doing. Two pairs of skinny legs were already dangling over the edge, and before I could tell them to take it slow, a third pair of legs appeared.

We were still one math nerd short.

I stepped back, and there was Munch. He was still standing on the ledge, his shoulders wedged against the wall. If he was trying to impersonate a statue, he was doing a great job.

I cupped my hands around my mouth. "Hey, Munch!" I whispered. When he didn't budge, I tried again: "Listen, you don't have to come with us, but you can't stay on that ledge. Just go back the way you came!"

I barely had a chance to finish before a flashlight flickered on in Cabin Gamma's nearby window. Now he was hemmed in on both sides.

Graham landed in a heap of arms and legs, but he popped back up at once. "You can do it, Munch. We'll catch you."

Marshane landed next to Graham. "Are you crazy?" he replied as he got back to his feet. "How are *we* gonna catch *him*?"

Graham glared at Marshane. "Well, we can't just leave him up there."

I stepped between Graham and Marshane as Oliver hit the ground. "You two need to *shut up*." Then I set my sights on Munch. "Listen, Munch, we'll talk you through it. All you have to do is get down on your hands and knees, then ease yourself over the edge. Once your arms are fully extended, it's only, like, a three-foot drop."

This was a bald-faced lie—it was more like a four-foot drop, and that was only if you were as tall as I was—but that didn't seem worth mentioning.

I was looking for a way to climb back up when Munch finally made a move. He popped something in his mouth—it looked like a fun-size Snickers—and squeezed his wide eyes shut. I was trying to decide if he was savoring the candy or sending up a last-minute prayer when a flicker of movement caught my eye. The silhouette was getting bigger.

Graham and Marshane had noticed, too. "It's now or never," Graham whispered at the same time Marshane said, "You're running out of time, Fun Size."

I flicked Marshane in the ear. "Don't pay any attention to them, Munch. You've got to get down on all fours, then find something to hold on to."

He waited for an extra second, then got down on his hands and knees. I couldn't help but be relieved.

"Now you have to lower yourself down," I said. "Then you just have to let go."

"I just have to let *go*?" Munch squeaked.

"We'll catch you, won't we, Graham?" When Graham didn't answer, I elbowed him. "*Won't* we?"

Graham licked his lips. "Uh-huh."

While Munch mustered his courage, my eyes flickered back and forth between the outline in the window, which was fumbling with the drapes, and Munch's quaking legs, which were still dangling from the ledge. A crinkly wrapper floated down, glinting silver in the moonlight. If he didn't speed this up, we were going to get caught.

"Go *now*," I said through gritted teeth. "Munch, you have to go right now!"

As soon as I got the last word out, Munch let go of the ledge. Graham and I scrambled to catch him, but Marshane was in the way. Munch landed right on top of him; he couldn't have hit him any better if Marshane had had a bull's-eye painted on top of his head.

They went down in a clump of arms and legs and fun-size wrappers. Marshane started to howl, but I clapped a hand over his mouth. The sliding door was sliding.

I seized Munch's sleeve and dragged him and Marshane underneath the ledge. Luckily, Graham and Oliver had the good sense to follow us. One second passed, then two, then ten, and it was all that I could do not to make a single sound. Finally, the sliding door slammed shut, and the drapes went still again.

I released a held-in breath and let go of Munch's sleeve. Oliver fell, gasping. A bead of sweat rolled down my nose and dripped into the flower bed.

Graham massaged his chest. "Why are we doing this again?"

"To stop a killer," I said darkly.

Munch struggled to sit up. "Oh, is that what we've been doing?"

"Funny," Marshane said, "I thought we've been clobbering each other."

I rubbed the sweat out of my eyes. "Come on," I said tiredly as I led them toward the storage room.

After everything we'd just been through, getting past the window was a breeze. While Oliver double-checked the lock—he certainly was a skittish one—Graham and I rearranged the boxes to create a makeshift fort. When I flicked my flashlight on, the math nerds huddled around it like a roaring campfire.

"I'm gonna give it to you straight," I said once everyone was settled. "What I'm about to say could be dangerous and maybe even deadly, so if you'd rather bow out now, no one will think any less of you."

This was another bald-faced lie—I'd definitely think less of them if they scuttled out that window with their tails between their legs—but if it would get rid of a few of them, I was prepared to sing and dance. Unfortunately, no one moved. Their faces gleamed in the flashlight like perfectly polished coins, some with excitement, some with fear. Oliver looked like he might barf (and since we'd just had lasagna, it wasn't going to be a pretty sight), but he managed not to blow.

I drew a deep breath, then pulled the note out of my pocket. "If you have one of the clues, now's the time to get it out."

The math nerds hesitated, but when I smoothed out my

note and set it next to the flashlight, they slowly pulled out theirs. Except Graham and Oliver were the only ones with clues.

I slugged Marshane in the shoulder. "I thought you said you guys had clues!"

"Oliver does," Marshane replied. "I was with him when he found it. And Munch was with Graham when he found *us*."

I knotted my arms across my waist. They weren't supposed to be involved. More math nerds equaled more targets.

Graham held up his hands. "What was I supposed to tell them?"

"You weren't supposed to tell them anything." I shone the flashlight at my note. "Did you think this was a game?"

The math nerds leaned over the note, their wide eyes flicking back and forth as they rushed to take it in.

"What's a manticore?" Munch asked before they were even halfway through.

"A beast," Oliver said. "Lion's body, scorpion's tail. Definitely not a household pet."

Munch shuddered. "What's a sphinx?"

"Lion's body, human's face."

Marshane threw up his arms. "Will you at least let us finish reading before we have to do vocabulary?"

Munch let them finish reading.

Graham must have finished first, because he was the first one to lean back and scratch the back of his head. "Oh, man, that's . . ."

"Messed up," Marshane finished.

I nodded ruefully. Graham set the two clues side by side:

```
Satyr and Minotaur share a cabin with two
other monsters.

Siren has a nickname.
```

Neither said much on its own, and they didn't say a lot when they were smooshed together, either. But I didn't want to say that. What if I was missing something?

Thankfully, Graham said it for me: "If there's an answer, I don't see it."

"Me neither," Munch admitted.

"Me neither," I admitted, too.

Oliver took a step back. "Maybe there isn't an answer because there isn't a problem." When we just stood there gaping, he added not-so-patiently, "Maybe they're faking us out."

My thoughts instantly leaped to the Fenimore Forger, who also had a nasty habit of faking naive people out. But before I could get *more* worked up than I already was, Marshane batted that away.

"Or maybe we just need more clues."

"We'll keep an eye out," Graham replied.

"No, *I'll* keep an eye out." I pointed a thumb at my chest. "I was the one who found the note, so I'm the one who should solve it."

Marshane rolled his eyes. "Stop trying to sacrifice yourself. The killer probably knows we found these clues, so we're in as deep as you are."

I opened my mouth to answer, then snapped it shut again. Marshane was right. Whether I wanted their help or not, they *were* in as deep as I was. The killer had made certain of that.

CHAPTER 9

After I jotted down the clues and a few ideas in my sketch-book, we left the storage room in shifts, first Graham, then Marshane, then Munch and Oliver, then me. Graham had tried to get me to go first—he'd even called me a lady—but I wanted to make sure we left everything exactly as we'd found it. After rearranging the boxes and double-checking the window, I returned my flashlight to my pocket and eased the door shut on my heels. I braced myself for impact as I tip-toed up the hall, but the common room was empty. The mess hall was empty, too.

I tiptoed up the stairs and scurried over the first bridge, each step less cautious than the last. We'd outwitted the killer *and* Director Verity. But no sooner had I slipped into Cabin Epsilon than someone fumbled with the light switch.

Not that the lights turned on, of course.

"That would have been much more dramatic if the power weren't still out."

I whirled around despite myself. Angeline was looming over me in pink pinstriped pajamas. How she managed to loom when she was barely taller than a garden gnome, I had no idea.

"Where have *you* been?" she demanded.

I glanced down at my jeans, which were caked with mud and bits of tree bark, then back up at Angeline. "I guess you won't believe I was looking for a midnight snack?"

"Since it's just ten thirty, no."

Brooklyn rolled over in bed. "If you two yahoos don't shut up, then I'm going to eat *you*."

Angeline ignored her. "You've got three seconds to spill." She wiggled her eyebrows. "Did you sneak out with the boys?"

I felt my cheeks get hot. "Not quite."

She yanked me down onto her bed. "Tell me everything," she said.

I dusted bits of tree bark off my jeans while I decided what to tell her. I'd already exposed half of the math nerds by letting them in on the secret. It seemed stupid to expose another. But a part of me—a stronger part—wanted her to believe me.

Ignoring the rumbling in my stomach, I pulled out my sketchbook and silently handed it to her. She took it without saying a word and calmly flipped through the clues until she landed on my note. I could tell when she got to the end, because she snapped the sketchbook shut.

"Where did you find these?" she demanded.

I couldn't help but blink. "I found the note down by the truck. We found Graham's clue in the sitting room during Mr. Pearson's workshop. I don't know where they found Oliver's, but he or Munch could tell you. Or maybe Marshane was with him?"

"Who's Munch?" Angeline asked.

"I don't know his real name," I admitted, "but he's the one who likes Swiss Rolls. Oh, and I call Wyatt 'Whistler' for, you know, obvious reasons." When she batted that away and leaped off the bed, I asked, "Do you know what's going on?"

"Who cares?" Brooklyn replied. "Now, will you *please* shut up? Some of us are trying to get some sleep."

If Brooklyn was using the word "please," she was deadly serious. Angeline must have thought so, too, because she lowered her voice.

"There's an old legend," she said, "about the man who owned these woods."

The hair on the back of my neck prickled. "Yeah, Munch mentioned him," I said.

Angeline nodded knowingly. "The man's name was Archimedes, and he was a brilliant mathematician. Some say he was a professor who took the ancient thinker's name after he found another way to calculate the value of pi, and some say he *was* Archimedes, who somehow used mathematics to unnaturally extend his life."

Brooklyn huffed under her breath.

Angeline managed to ignore her. "According to the legend, he challenged the mountain man Jim Bridger to a water-hauling contest. Whoever could get the most water from Lake Wannacrunchanumber to the top of Lookout Hill would win the deed to all the land. Mr. Bridger took the bet, confident in his superiority, but Archimedes never intended to compete with the mountain man's muscles. While Mr. Bridger spent the day hauling bucket after bucket, Archimedes built a simple screw pump. He moved more water in ten minutes than Mr. Bridger had in ten hours, and just like that, the deed was his."

I couldn't help but shiver. I'd never been the superstitious sort, but I'd never been trapped at a math camp with a homicidal maniac. Suddenly, it felt like my sketchbook was on fire.

"But Archimedes must be dead," I said. "If he won it from Jim Bridger, he can't still be alive—right?"

Now that my eyes had adjusted, I could see Angeline more clearly. Her solemn eyes and hollow cheeks looked like they'd been carved from stone. "I don't know," she said. "Someone had to leave that note."

When I woke up the next morning, Angeline's last words were still rattling around in my head: *Someone had to leave that note. Someone had to leave that note. Someone had to leave . that note.* I jammed my head under my pillow, but the chant only got louder. I was still trying to ignore it when the flesh-and-blood Angeline dragged the blanket off my legs with another of her awkward arm-wave moves.

"Rise and shine!" she chirped. "I have something to show you."

At least that caught my attention. Grudgingly, I climbed out of bed and dug a pair of cargo shorts out of my duffel. The jeans I'd been wearing yesterday were officially toast. I'd wiggled out of them before I'd tumbled into bed, and they were still standing up in the corner, a sculpture in mud and denim. It really was too bad Director Saffron wouldn't see it.

I was headed down the hall when I spied a scrap of paper, thin and smooth like all the others, poking up out of a gap between the floorboards and the wall. My stomach did a somersault as I bent down to retrieve. Sure enough, it was a clue:

```
Hydra and Cyclops are involved in a not-
so-secret fling.
```

I quickly checked both ways, but whoever had planted the clue had already disappeared. Sighing, I wadded it up and shoved it deep into my pocket. If I ignored the killer's clues, maybe he'd leave me alone.

By the time I made it down to breakfast, Angeline had disappeared. Apparently, what she'd wanted to show me wasn't as urgent as I'd thought. I tried not to feel annoyed as I sat down across from Toby, who was chewing his last bite. An uneaten plate of pork links was sitting by his elbow.

"They were almost out," he said, nudging the plate across the table, "so I thought I'd get you some."

After last night's drama, this small act of kindness was enough to make me sniffle. "Thanks, Toby," I said.

He took a swig of coffee. Then he took another swig. "Anything you want to talk about?"

I hemmed and hawed uncomfortably. Toby tended to leave the hard-core parenting to Mom, but then, she was out of reach.

"No," I finally said, dragging a hand under my nose. As much as I wanted to dump the whole twisted tale on him, I wasn't going to expose him any more than I already had.

He tipped his head toward Mr. Sharp. "Gordon's pretty sure he can jerry-rig the truck, but even if he can't, he offered to drive us down to Morgan." He drained his coffee in one gulp. "I guess they have a shuttle there that makes runs to Camp Vermeer."

"We're leaving?" I asked stupidly.

Toby's forehead crinkled. "I thought you wanted to leave."

I *did* want to leave. But I also wanted to find out what these clues were pointing toward. If something happened to these kids, I would blame myself forever. They might have been math nerds, but they'd quickly become *my* math nerds.

"I do," I said indignantly. "It's just that I'm kind of involved in this kind-of-crucial project, and the session's halfway over, anyway—"

"So you want to stay," he said. It wasn't quite a question, but it might as well have been.

"No!" I couldn't help but blurt. I cleared my throat and tried again: "I mean, *no*, I can't stay *here*. We never paid the fees. They might not have enough supplies."

Toby frowned. "Fair point."

I practically sagged with relief. He hadn't figured me out yet. "So Camp Vermeer or bust?" I asked.

He pressed his lips into a line. They disappeared into his beard. "Sure, Camp Vermeer or bust," he said.

Before I had a chance to redirect our conversation, a nearby scuffle caught my eye. Angeline had reappeared in the middle of the breakfast line—literally in the middle, right in front of Brooklyn—and Brooklyn wasn't budging. I expected Angeline to yield, but she stayed right in Brooklyn's face.

"Back off, Barbie," Brooklyn growled.

I couldn't hear Angeline's reply, but Brooklyn didn't take her bait, just tried to worm her way around her.

Angeline wasn't finished yet. "Hey, Brooklyn," she said, scooping up a spoonful of grape jam.

When Brooklyn turned around, Angeline lobbed it at her head.

The first thing I felt was glee. It might have been cruel and petty, but I'd wanted to see Brooklyn get what was coming to her since she'd nearly knocked my block off. The next thing I felt was disbelief. I blinked and rubbed my eyes, but when I opened them again, Brooklyn was still seething, and Angeline was still smirking. I was beginning to think that time had figured out how to stand still when Angeline scooped up another spoonful. Then Ms. Gutierrez sprang between them.

Then the director came out of her office.

"ANGELINE!" she barked after taking one look at the scene.

Angeline lowered her arm, but the damage was already done. The grape jam rolled down Brooklyn's cheek and splatted loudly on the floor.

The mess hall was so silent that I could hear Munch chewing and the fire crackling. Only Mr. Pearson, who was calmly tending to his scones, seemed immune to the shock wave.

Director Verity swallowed. "Get cleaned up," she told Brooklyn, then set her sights on Angeline. For a long time she just stood there glaring. If she'd been angry before, she was downright livid now. "And you just—you just—go to your room, and don't come out until I tell you to come out!"

Brooklyn ducked into the bathroom on the far side of the mess hall, but Angeline held her ground. I fought the urge to rub my eyes. I was missing something here. There was something I wasn't seeing. But I couldn't work it out before Angeline trashed her spoon and made a beeline for the stairs.

If one of us was going to go ballistic, I wouldn't have guessed it would be her.

The director sighed. "My apologies for the theatrics." She motioned toward the mess. "Mr. Sharp, Ms. Gutierrez, would you mind cleaning that up? I have some business to attend to."

As Director Verity clicked away, I felt my chest slowly deflate. Everyone else deflated, too. Forks clinked, voices hummed, and a pair of dishrags hit the floorboards with an unsettling splat.

Toby tried to take a sip of coffee, then remembered it was gone and grimly set the mug back down. "Things are getting kind of weird."

"You have no idea," I muttered, shoving the pork links away.

As soon as breakfast was over, Director Verity returned. Apparently, the awful weather was turning us into wound-up springs, so we were going to run around the gym until we came to our senses.

Though the math nerds lodged complaints, I was secretly excited. Some good old-fashioned exercise was just what I needed to get my head in the right place. Except good old-fashioned exercise produced good old-fashioned sweat, so in an hour, maybe more, I was in desperate need of a shower and another set of clothes. The thought of talking to Angeline, who was still a wound-up spring, wasn't exactly a nice one, but since I'd have to face her now or later, it might as well be now.

It took me ten whole minutes to scrape together enough courage, but when I pushed open that door, the only thing that greeted me was a cold, abandoned room.

Angeline was gone.

CHAPTER 10

I tightened my grip on the knob. Angeline was gone. After I'd told her about the note. After she'd told *me* about the legend.

I forced myself to breathe. There were ninety-seven places she could be at that moment, and ninety-six of them were more boring than Math Genius. It was too early to freak out.

I flipped the light switch out of habit and was surprised when it turned on. The power must have started working while we were stinking up the gym. But I wouldn't celebrate until I found Angeline.

First, I checked behind the door. Then I checked under the bunks. When cold air curled around my ankles, my gaze darted to the sliding door, which was slightly open. I scrambled to my feet and shoved the blinds out of the way, but the balcony was as empty as the rest of Cabin Epsilon.

A shiver skittered down my spine, but I pretended not to notice as I closed the sliding door. There had to be an explanation, and it was up to me to find it.

I was out the door in a few steps and down the hall in a few more. I was passing Cabin Gamma when the door whipped open from the inside and I crashed into Marshane.

"Hey, watch it!" he barked, then glanced at me over his shoulder. "Oh, hey, Esther. What's up?"

"Have you seen Angeline?" I asked.

He shook his head. "Not since this morning."

I kicked the door frame. "Drat!"

One corner of his mouth curled up. "Is that a substitute swear word or some kind of mutant rodent?"

I scowled. "Don't start with me." I glanced over the railing, but she wasn't in the game room, either.

Marshane's eyes lit up. "Is this about—?"

"Don't say it," I cut in, sneaking peeks in both directions. "You never know who might be listening."

"Do you want me to help you look?"

"If it will shut you up," I said.

At the bottom of the stairs, I pointed my chin toward the game room. "If you go that way, I'll go this way." I slid my phone out of my pocket. "We'll meet back here in ten minutes."

"Why ten minutes?" he replied. "And if I'm not back for our meeting, will you send out the search party for me, too?"

I scowled again. "Just do it!"

He had the nerve to salute. "Whatever you say, ma'am." And with that, he sauntered off.

I didn't wait for him to vanish, just set my sights on the mess hall. It was all that I could do not to break into a sprint and scour the lodge from top to bottom, but if the killer was watching, then I had to play this cool.

After circling the mess hall, I crept into the common room, where Mr. Sharp and Ms. Gutierrez were leading a rowdy game of Sevens. At first, I hovered near the back, but when I didn't catch a glimpse of Angeline, I sat down next to Munch. "Have you seen Angeline?" I asked.

Munch nearly leaped out of his seat. "Are you trying to give a guy a heart attack?"

"Sorry," I mumbled. "I'm just trying to find Angeline."

Munch's forehead crinkled. "She got banished, didn't she?"

"Yeah, she did," I said. "But she isn't in our room." I turned to go, then turned right back. "If you happen to run into her, will you let her know I'm looking for her?"

"Yeah, sure," he said absently. It looked like Sevens had already recaptured his attention.

I slipped out of the common room as silently as I'd slipped in. The hall that led down to the storage rooms was silent and shadowy, much like the storage rooms themselves. I was so paranoid that I kept checking behind me—which was how

I crashed into a wall. But then the wall harrumphed, and I realized it wasn't a wall.

It was Mr. Pearson's chest.

"I'm so sorry!" I leaped back. He didn't seem like the sort of person who'd overlook people crashing into him, and I'd crashed into him *twice*. It was time to smooth things over. "Were you playing basketball?"

Mr. Pearson's eyes narrowed. "I could ask you the same thing."

It took me a few seconds to realize that I might be in trouble. "Oh, I was just playing Sevens with Mr. Sharp and Ms. Gutierrez, but then I realized that Angeline wasn't there, and since I haven't seen her since, you know, I figured I should try to find her."

The words poured out of me faster than I'd meant them to, and for a moment, I was sure Mr. Pearson would see through me. But instead of grilling me, he scowled.

"Well, she isn't here," he said, "so I suggest you take your search elsewhere."

"Good idea," I said breathlessly, spinning around and scurrying off. I didn't stop to catch my breath until I'd nearly reached the stairs, where I almost tripped over a pair of familiar feet.

"Well?" I asked Marshane, planting both hands on my knees.

He tucked his hands behind his head. "I found a

calculator in the game room, a graphic novel in the sitting room, and an inhaler on the stairs." He pulled a lipstick from his pocket. "Oh, and I found *this* in the theater."

"There's a theater?" I asked.

"Oh, yeah," Marshane replied. "It's got recliners, stadium seating, all the latest bells and whistles. But aren't you at least *curious* about whose lipstick this is?" He returned it to his pocket. "I think Ms. Gutierrez is involved with Mr. Sharp. Mr. Pearson is too creepy to be involved with *anyone*."

I couldn't have cared less about that stupid tube of lipstick. "What about Angeline?" I asked.

Marshane's wiry shoulders drooped. "Yeah, no sign of her," he said.

I felt my shoulders droop, too. "Then I guess we have no choice."

"No choice but to do *what*?" he replied.

I pressed my lips into a line. "Talk to Director Verity."

Before he could talk me out of it, I squared my sagging shoulders and marched back across the mess hall. Mr. Sharp and Ms. Gutierrez were still in the middle of their game, so I only just tapped on her door. I didn't want to make a scene.

Luckily, she answered before I had to knock again. "What may I help you with?" she asked, then took a closer look at me. "Esther, what is it? You look like you've just seen Euler's ghost."

I drew a bracing breath. If I told her, it was possible that she'd think I was crazy. But if I *didn't* tell her, it was possible that Angeline would never be heard from again.

"It's Angeline," I said. "I can't find her anywhere."

Director Verity relaxed. "You don't need to worry about Angeline. I've already taken care of her."

She'd already *taken care of her*? I was still trying to decide how to respond to that announcement when Director Verity went on.

"I probably should have told you sooner, but I'm afraid Angeline left. When I spoke to her grandfather this morning, he and I agreed it would be best to cut her visit short."

An alarm bell went off in my head. "But the phones don't work up here."

She gestured over her shoulder. "Oh, I have a satellite phone. It's not the sleekest piece of tech, but it does get the job done."

Another alarm bell went off in my head. "But what about the road? It's been, like, washed out for days. How could an old man drive up it?"

"It's getting clearer all the time. Besides, Angeline's grand-father used to be a forest ranger, so he's accustomed to these mountains, not to mention these conditions." When I just stood there blinking, Director Verity added, "Oh, and he's got four-wheel drive."

She was lying through her lipstick, but there was no way I could prove it. And until I found some evidence, there was no way I could prove that Angeline had been kidnapped. But something was definitely up.

Maybe Director Verity had left that note herself.

I stepped back instinctively and bumped into Marshane. I hadn't noticed him creep up behind me, but I was grateful that he had.

Director Verity stepped forward. "Are you sure you're all right? If you've been feeling poorly, I could ask Mr. Pearson to whip up some lemon tea."

I shook my head. "No, I'm all right." The last thing I wanted to do was let her *or* Mr. Pearson anywhere near me. "I think I just need a break."

"Then you should take one," she replied, slamming the door shut in my face.

That was a fine how-do-you-do. Did she have some-thing—or some*one*—incriminating in her office?

Marshane cleared his throat. "Are you gonna keep step-ping on my foot?"

I glanced down at his foot (which I was definitely step-ping on). "Tell the others we need to meet," I said as I headed for the stairs. "Before dinner, you know where."

"What are you gonna do in the meantime?"

"Reconnaissance," I said.

I figured I had a few minutes before the game of Sevens broke up, so I needed to search Cabin Epsilon while Brooklyn was distracted. If I couldn't find Angeline, at least I could find evidence.

After making sure the room was as secure as I could make it, I scoured Angeline's bunk. I hadn't noticed earlier, but the puffy pink blanket was gone, replaced by a wad of crumpled sheets. It certainly looked like she'd gone home, but then, looks could be deceiving.

I used my practice foil, which I'd crammed into my duffel before Toby and I left, to separate the pale blue sheets, then picked through them one by one. She wouldn't have gone without a fight, so there was a good chance they'd left forensic evidence behind. But after digging through each sheet, I couldn't find signs of a struggle. There was no blood, no intestines, and the only hairs in sight were Angeline's long blond ones.

After drop-kicking her pillow across the room in frustration, I clambered up the ladder and inspected the top bunk. It looked exactly like my bunk had looked on my first day at camp. Sighing, I hopped off the ladder and got down on my hands and knees. Maybe she'd heard the killer coming and tried to hide under the bed. But the only things under the bed were a warren of dust bunnies and a lonely ankle sock.

I sank back against the wall, ready to admit defeat. The more I questioned Director Verity's story, the more it seemed to check out.

I let my gaze wander as I fiddled with the ankle sock. In murder mysteries, like in life, it was all about perspective. Brooklyn's bunk was undisturbed, and my bed looked no different than it had this morning. Then I noticed that the closet door was slightly ajar.

I wouldn't have even known it was a closet if I hadn't caught a glimpse of hangers. There were only two or three, like we weren't expected to unpack. But as I scrambled to my feet, I could tell that *something* was in the closet. And as soon as I opened the door, I knew exactly what it was: Angeline's pink duffel.

Pinned to the shoulder strap was another typewritten clue.

CHAPTER 11

Centaur, Griffin, Unicorn, and Manticore
share a cabin.

As far as clues went, it was harmless. Still, I couldn't decide whether to scream or celebrate. If Angeline had really left, she would have taken her stuff with her.

And if there weren't a killer, he wouldn't have left his calling card.

I stuffed the clue into my pocket, but I left the rest alone. I didn't want to tamper with forensic evidence.

For the rest of the day, that scrap of paper weighed me down. It was always there, taunting and tormenting me, a small but serious reminder of how I'd failed Angeline. As soon as I could reasonably call it "before dinner," I snuck up to the girls' bathroom.

I was halfway out the window when a low voice hissed, "Hey, Esther!"

I immediately ducked for cover and was racking my brains for an explanation when I realized that the voice had actually come from below me—and that it belonged to Munch. He was hanging out the window of the lodge's first-floor bathroom.

"It was *my* idea," he said as he wriggled out the window. "Don't you think it was a good one?"

It *was* a good idea, but that was beside the point. If he kept yapping like a purse dog, we were going to get caught. I pressed a finger to my lips.

"Oh, they won't hear us," he replied, giving the wall a solid whack. "These logs are super-thick."

Shut up! I wanted to shout, but since that would only make it worse, I pressed my lips into a line. Munch waited patiently beneath the ledge while I lowered myself down, then offered me some Fruit Roll-Ups. I accepted eagerly. Fruit Roll-Ups were my favorite bribe.

After climbing through the window, I licked off my sticky fingers and surveyed the math nerds as a whole. "I'm sure you know by now that Angeline's gone missing, but what you might not know is that I got a cryptic note"—I paused to let that sink in—"which means that there's a chance, a good chance, that Angeline's in trouble."

Oliver snorted to himself. When I glared in his direction, he clapped a hand over his mouth, but the damage was already done. If he thought I was insane, he should have mustered up the courage to admit it to my face.

I was about to challenge him when Munch frowned and shook his head. "I heard she got kicked out," he said.

Marshane tipped his head at me. "Brooklyn didn't get kicked out after she nearly decked *her*."

"And *if* she got kicked out, why'd she leave her stuff?" I asked, pulling the latest clue out of my pocket. Oliver would have to wait. "And why'd I find this clue pinned to her duffel's shoulder strap?"

No one could answer that.

Graham tilted his head to the side. "Could she still be in the lodge? I mean, it *is* pretty huge."

"We've already scoured every inch and can't find her anywhere."

"Could she be down by the lake?"

"Or the amphitheater?" Munch asked.

We hadn't checked the lake (and I hadn't even heard of the amphitheater), but they were missing the big picture.

"Why would she go out?" I asked. "And even if she did, why wouldn't she come back?"

Once again, they had no answer. An unsettling silence descended on the storage room, like an itch you couldn't reach. But I was right. I knew I was. Just because they couldn't see it didn't mean it wasn't true.

"What about the cabin?" Munch replied as he produced some more Fruit Roll-Ups.

"What cabin?" I demanded.

He shoved them into his mouth. "Oh, you know, the creepy cabin at the top of Lookout Hill." He swallowed the whole thing in one wad. "I heard it belonged to Archimedes."

I crinkled my forehead. Ghosts didn't need cabins. "But isn't he, like, dead?"

"Maybe," Munch admitted. "But there *is* a cabin up there, and I've seen it for myself."

I shone the flashlight in his eyes. "You're not just playing us, are you?"

"Why would I play you?" he replied. "Oliver and I got up here early, before it really started raining, so we decided to explore."

"*Munch* decided to explore," Oliver added for good measure. "He forced me to come along."

My salivary glands froze up. "Could you find your way up there again?"

"Could Isaac Newton take derivatives?"

I decided to take that as a yes.

CHAPTER 12

We called it Operation Newton so it wouldn't sound suspicious if one of the counselors overheard. Munch didn't want to go until it was fully dark, so we agreed to fake lights-out, then sneak back out around 10:30, once the counselors had made their rounds. I was supposed to meet them by the storage room's window, and then they were supposed to show me how to get to Archimedes's cabin.

I would have preferred a daytime op—it was going to be too dark to look for bloodstains—but it was probably better this way. So far, we'd managed to avoid detection, but if three of us went missing in the middle of a workshop, the director would have noticed.

While Brooklyn got ready for bed, I pretended to get ready, too. I brushed my teeth for five whole minutes while she meticulously flossed and gargled, then tailed her back to Cabin Epsilon and changed into my pajamas. She didn't say one word to me, and I didn't say one word to her, but as we climbed into bed, I couldn't help but peep, "Good night."

She didn't bother to respond, just harrumphed and rolled over. That was probably just as well. If I started to act weird, Brooklyn might start to suspect.

I waited for her breathing to even out, then for Mr. Pearson's footsteps to drag up and down the hall. They might have been Mr. Sharp's or Ms. Gutierrez's, but I thought the shuffling gait fit him. He reminded me of a zombie.

Once the footsteps came and went, I counted to three hundred and eight, then slowly folded back my blanket, slid my feet into my shoes, and tiptoed over to the door. The knob stuck when I tried to turn it, so I had to turn it harder, and the door actually squealed. I snuck a peek over my shoulder, but Brooklyn was still snoozing peacefully. She hadn't moved a muscle. Allowing myself a tiny sigh, I eased the door open a crack and padded out into the hall.

I wasted no time in reaching the main floor. The mess hall's lights were off, but the embers smoldering in the fireplace produced just enough light that I could cross the dining room without running into anything. A narrow strip of light was shining under Director Verity's door, so I was extra careful as I tiptoed past her office. Apparently, lights-out didn't apply to the director.

The common room was cold and dark, as was the wider corridor. When I got to the bathroom, I knocked on the door once, then twice, then three times—the secret password we'd worked out so we wouldn't accidentally walk in on someone *using* the bathroom—then opened it when no one answered. The air in the bathroom was at least ten degrees cooler than the air in the corridor, but that was probably because someone had left the window open.

We would have to have a talk about covering our tracks.

I shimmied out the window and dropped into another flower bed. Munch and Oliver were already waiting for me, though they were hunched under the window that led to the storage room.

"What are you doing?" I whispered.

"Trying to read this clue," Munch said as he stepped out of the way. "Someone tacked it to the windowsill."

Anxiety churned in my stomach. I tore it off its nail and tromped around the nearest corner. After looking left, then right, I cupped my hands around my flashlight and read the clue through my fingers:

Phoenix wears glasses.

I crinkled my nose. "How'd he know we'd use the windows?"

"They *were* open," Munch replied.

I glanced up at Lookout Hill. "Or maybe he knows we're getting close."

I waited for Oliver to snort, but this time, he almost shivered. His self-preservation instinct must have been (finally) kicking in.

"We'd better get going," Munch replied as he handed me the clue. "Marshane convinced our other roommate that we're just raiding the kitchen, but we still can't take *too* long."

I fell into step behind him, leaving Oliver to fall into step behind me. He hadn't wanted to come with us, but I'd more or less insisted. If Munch got lost or turned around, we would need Oliver's opinion.

Though the circumstances could have been less serious, it felt good to be outside again, stretching my legs, breathing fresh air. We'd been cooped up in that lodge for what felt like a century.

As the trees inched closer, a narrow road appeared, but Munch didn't bother to take it, just ducked beneath the nearest trees. It was darker under here, and the ground was less even, but we didn't dare to use the flashlight. Creepy cabins in the woods always belonged to serial killers, and the last thing we wanted to do was alert him to our presence.

When the ground became uneven, I knew that we'd reached the hill. I felt more than saw it rise, and with every step I took, my legs got heavier. We were on some sort of path, but it was littered with debris—twigs, deer droppings, you name it. By the time the trees started to thin, my shins were officially on fire. When I tripped over a tree root, I had to grab a nearby bush, and when my toe caught on a rock, I nearly bowled Munch over.

"How much—farther?" I asked between noisy gasps for breath.

Oliver shushed me, but Munch pointed at a shaft of moonlight.

"There," he said so softly his voice might have been a breeze.

Ignoring the burning in my shins, I stumbled past the last few bushes, then instantly jolted to a stop. The shaft of moonlight he'd been pointing at was a break in the trees. It flooded a small clearing, highlighting the ramshackle cabin.

Compared to the lodge, it was a shack. The walls made me think of giant Lincoln Logs that had survived six kids, and the roof was losing its fight with gravity (if it had ever been winning in the first place). Though what looked like a single lightbulb burned behind the picture window, the place looked barely inhabitable. If a serial killer didn't live here, I didn't know who would.

Munch crouched down beside me. "We tried to scope it out, but we could see this gnarly silhouette when we were up here a few days ago. It looked like a shotgun."

I craned my neck. "A shotgun?" Only crazies owned shotguns.

He motioned toward the picture window. "We could see the outline through the drapes."

I forced myself not to shiver. "Come on," I said through gritted teeth. "We've got to get closer."

Oliver shrank back against the trees. "Are you kidding?" he replied. "What if someone catches us?"

"Who's gonna catch us?" I replied. "You think this whole thing is a joke."

He sent me a dirty look. He was cornered, and he knew it. At least he had the dignity to let our silly squabble go.

"All right, then, who's coming with me?"

Oliver lowered his gaze. I arched an eyebrow at him, but otherwise, I didn't react. If they were going to be wusses, they were going to be wusses. I wasn't going to force them. I was about to continue on alone when Munch finally raised his hand.

"I am," he replied.

His voice might have cracked, but at least he'd volunteered. I had to give him props for that.

"We don't have time to run surveillance, so we're gonna have to take this slow." I surveyed the cabin one more time. "For now, let's stick to the perimeter, then pull back and regroup. But if you find an entrance to a basement, definitely let me know."

Munch licked off his fingers. "Get in, find a basement, and get out."

"And *don't* get caught," I said.

"I think I can handle that."

I glanced at Oliver. "Unless you want to hike back by yourself, you might as well act as our lookout. And try not to pee your pants if Archimedes shows his face."

He stuck both hands on his hips. "I have *never* peed my pants."

I seriously doubted that. "Good for you," was all I said.

After checking and rechecking our supplies (which basically amounted to flicking my flashlight on and off), Munch and I set out. The clearing wasn't clear of grass, so at least we had some cover. It scratched my cheeks and clawed at my socks as we half scuttled, half galloped around one of the edges. I would have loved to draw it—the fibrous texture would have involved crosshatching, my favorite—but creeping through it was a drag. I stuck out an arm when we reached the narrow road, then checked both ways and raced across it, dragging Munch along behind me. When we reached the other side, I pulled him down into a crouch, but as far as I could tell, we hadn't been spotted. The drapes hadn't even twitched.

It didn't take us long to reach the edge of the grass. The cabin huddled in a ring of dirt, a clearing within a clearing. I stuck out my arm again, but it was probably overkill. The cabin might as well have been a tomb. Maybe Archimedes had skipped town without turning off his lights.

I paused for one more second, then motioned toward a corner on the far side of the house. We couldn't assume he wasn't there unless we wanted to get caught. Munch must have agreed, because he made a break for it before I had to tell him twice. As soon as he reached the corner, I skedaddled after him.

Munch and I made a good team. While I peered into every window, he inspected the foundation, searching for an entrance to a basement, but we both struck out. These windows had drapes, too, and the foundation wasn't even cracked.

Then another light turned on.

Munch and I exchanged a wide-eyed look—it was coming through the window just behind us—then dashed around the next corner and collapsed against the wall. I kept waiting for an old man to cuss us out in Greek, but the night air barely stirred. If the stars hadn't been twinkling and the crickets hadn't been chirping, I might have been able to convince myself that time was standing still.

I'd just noticed the mud that was seeping through my jeans when Munch jostled my arm and pointed at something to our right. On the far side of the cabin, a shed hid in the shadows.

Bingo.

We exchanged another wide-eyed look, then made a bee-line for the shed. My pulse was pounding in my ears as I reached for the door handle—then discovered it was locked. And the padlock looked much sturdier than the one I'd bought for gym.

For the second time that day, I couldn't decide whether to scream or celebrate. On the one hand, it was locked, so we wouldn't be able to get in, but on the other, it was *locked*, which meant it was probably hiding something. Also, ghosts didn't lock doors, which meant that our mass murderer was of the flesh-and-blood variety. We'd have to find a pair of bolt cutters and come back another night. But when I signaled Munch to head back the way we'd come, he shook his head ferociously.

"I can pick the lock," he whispered.

"You can?" I whispered back.

He pointed a thumb at his chest. "Son of a locksmith," he said proudly.

I hunkered down beside the shed and wrapped my arms around my knees to keep my whole body from shaking. Was this really, truly it? Had Angeline been here all this time? Were we about to rescue her?

Munch was still picking the lock when something that sounded like a tiger—or a bunch of tigers—swarmed the hill. Munch and I shrank back against the shed, but before we could identify where the threat was coming from, a beam from a high-powered flashlight hit us right between the eyes.

"What in the name of Descartes are you doing?" an unexpected voice demanded.

CHAPTER 13

The director sighed. "For heaven's sake, Esther, it's the middle of the night!"

I raised a hand to shield my eyes, but I still couldn't see her face around the halo of the flashlight. At least I had the good sense not to answer her question. There was nothing I could say that wouldn't make me sound insane.

The flashlight swung over to Munch. "I'm surprised to see you here."

Munch's shoulders slumped, though I couldn't decide if he felt worse about getting caught or about being underestimated.

Director Verity aimed the flashlight back at me. "Well?" she asked indignantly. "What do you have to say for yourselves?"

I raised both hands to shield my eyes. "Could you turn that flashlight off? That thing's brighter than the sun."

Director Verity snorted like an angry rhinoceros, but at least she lowered her weapon. "Once we've safely vacated Dr. Rickman's property, you *will* explain yourselves."

With that, she whipped around and marched past Oliver (who'd been hovering behind her). She didn't wait for us to follow, but then, she didn't need to. Now that we'd been discovered, where were we going to go?

The camp's cherry-red truck was waiting at the clearing's edge. We climbed into the cab and nervously buckled our seat belts. The director didn't say a word as we jounced back down the road, just left us to our awful thoughts. I couldn't help but wonder what was going to happen to us—and, even worse, to Angeline.

When we trudged into the common room, Brooklyn leaped to her feet. She'd been doing a worksheet (for fun), but at the sight of us, she grinned. She must have been lying in her bunk, pretending not to be awake, when I snuck out earlier. I should have known it was a trick.

Brooklyn started to say something, but Director Verity cut her off.

"You may go back to bed now, Brooklyn."

The smile melted off her face. Apparently, she'd hoped to be a witness at our trial.

"I said, go back to bed." It was a command, not a suggestion. "The rest of you, stay where you are."

Brooklyn closed her mouth, then retreated toward the stairs, a crumpled piece of toilet paper trailing along behind her. If I'd been feeling slightly generous, I would have stomped on it to free it. *If* I'd been feeling slightly generous.

Once Brooklyn disappeared, Director Verity lined us up. I fought the urge to fidget as she wound her arms behind her back, then studied each of us in turn.

"Now," she finally said, "I want one of you to tell me what you were doing on Mr. Rickman's property, and I want you to tell me *now*." Her robe swirled around her ankles like a cape as she paced back and forth in front of us. "Esther? Moses? Oliver?"

I couldn't decide which I had a harder time believing, that Munch's real name was Moses or that Oliver hadn't cracked (yet).

Director Verity jerked to a stop. "I'm sure I don't have to tell you that the ground on which you stand literally belongs to Dr. Rickman."

At least that caught my attention. "I thought it belonged to Archimedes."

Director Verity's nostrils shriveled. "His first name is Archimedes, but as far as you're concerned, his name is Dr. Rickman. He's a mathematician of some influence . . . or at least he was." She raked a hand through her blond hair (which looked thin out of its bun). "Now you've disturbed his fragile peace."

"We're really sorry," Munch replied. "We really didn't mean to bug him."

"And it won't happen again," I said. Next time, we'd be more careful.

One corner of her mouth curled up. "It most certainly will *not*, because I'll be monitoring your free time for the remainder of the camp. Do I make myself clear?"

We dropped our eyes and mumbled, "Yeah."

"Very well," she said, massaging that squishy spot between her eyes. "You may return to bed now, too."

We shuffled up the stairs without mumbling another word. At least Director Verity had stopped asking us what we'd been doing. I would have lied if I'd had to, since Angeline's life was on the line, but I would have felt a little bad. Like I was going to feel bad when I broke into that shed.

One way or another, though, I was getting past that padlock.

As soon as I set foot in the mess hall the next morning, every eye zoomed in on me. Munch dipped his head, then returned his attention to his plate, but Oliver wouldn't stop glaring, and the other math nerds wouldn't stop staring. Even the counselors kept sneaking peeks in my direction when they thought I wasn't looking. In the space of a few hours, I'd gone back to being the outsider.

I fiddled with the skin around my elbow as I shuffled into the food line, careful not to make eye contact. Mr. Pearson had made omelets, but just the sight of all that goop was enough to make me sick. Instead of risking an explosion, I opted for a granola bar.

Director Verity didn't smile as I came up on the drinks station, but at least she didn't frown. "Good morning," she said evenly.

I took a bottled water. "Hey."

Director Verity arched an eyebrow. "I trust you got a good night's sleep?"

I felt my cheeks redden. "I guess."

"Excellent," she said, but it didn't sound like she meant it.

I glanced around the dining room. "Hey, have you seen Toby?" I desperately needed an ally.

She pressed her lips into a line. "Mr. Sharp and Mr. Renfro are busy working on the truck. Now that the weather has cleared up, I think your stepfather is hoping to—how do you kids put it? Blow this Popsicle stand?"

I winced. "Can I go out and talk to him?"

She looked me up and down. "I suppose," she finally said.

I set my bottled water down and made a break for the front door.

"But I expect you to be back for times table sprints!" she hollered after me.

I didn't bother to reply, just wrenched open the oak door and raised a hand to shield my eyes. For the first time in a long time, the sky was as bright blue as my favorite cobalt turquoise paint. I gave my eyes time to adjust, then surveyed the mucky driveway. Toby's beat-up truck was sitting right where we'd left it, and two pairs of hairy legs were sticking out from under it. Toby and Mr. Sharp had spread a tarp out on the ground, but they were still flecked with mud.

As I tramped down the steps, I got the eeriest sensation that I was being watched. A part of me wanted to bend down and use the railing as a shield, but with Toby and Mr. Sharp making enough noise to wake the dead, it wasn't like the killer didn't know right where we were.

"Hey, Toby," I said once I could say it without shouting.

His clanking missed a beat, but then it started up again. "Hey, Esther," he replied.

I dug my toe into the dirt. It was the consistency of cookie dough, damp but quickly drying out. I itched to sculpt something with it before it morphed back into dirt, but now was really *not* the time.

"I shouldn't have snuck out," I blurted at the same time Toby said, "I told Gordon not to worry about giving us a ride to Morgan."

I scrunched up my nose. "What?"

Toby's clanking didn't stop. "The truck is almost good to go . . ."

I could nearly hear the dot-dot-dot.

"And it seems like you've been having a good time with the number crunchers."

I huffed despite myself. "I'm *not* having a good time, I'm solving a very complex puzzle—"

I forced myself to stop before I said something problematic. Mr. Sharp wasn't my prime suspect, but I still couldn't rule him out.

"If you say so," Toby said. "And no, you really shouldn't have."

I scrunched up my nose again. "No, I really shouldn't have *what?*"

"Snuck out with the boys," he said.

I waited for him to continue, but of course, he held his peace. Toby never lectured, but then, he usually didn't have to.

The conversation dipped again. Only Toby's clanking and Mr. Sharp's grunting disturbed the uncertain silence. Their legs twitched as they strained to loosen one bolt or another, then, finally, went still.

"Why *did* you sneak out?" Toby asked. When I didn't answer right away, he slithered out from under the truck and squinted up at me. "You weren't . . . messing around with one of those number crunchers, were you?"

I felt my cheeks get hot, but before I could respond, Mr. Sharp slithered out, too, twisting his hands around his socket wrench.

"Just remembered I told Carmen that I'd help her with the cleanup"—he looked at me, then looked away—"so I guess I'll leave you to it."

He returned the socket wrench to his toolbox, then retreated to the lodge. I wanted to call after him, but my tongue wouldn't cooperate. By the time I untwisted it, he was already gone.

I kicked Toby's foot instead. "Are you kidding? That's disgusting." If I'd been feeling sick before, I was downright nauseated now.

Toby's shoulders sagged. "Well, that's something, anyway." He retrieved the socket wrench that Mr. Sharp had abandoned, then wriggled back under the truck. "So what were you guys doing?"

I fidgeted with my granola bar. Toby was as cool as grown-ups came, so I knew he wouldn't freak out. And since we were at a standstill, maybe it was time to bring a grown-up in.

"Well," I finally said, "it's just that I found this note."

But Toby had gone back to clanking. "What was that?" he asked.

"I said, I found this note!" I didn't mean to scream it, but I screamed it, anyway. After lowering my voice, I added, "It's from this guy named Sphinx."

"Who's Sphinx?" Toby replied.

"I don't know," I admitted. "I think that's kind of the point." I pulled the note out of my pocket—I'd started carrying it around—and carefully unfolded it. "It says that Sphinx is gonna kill someone."

"What was that?" he asked again.

Instead of answering, I got down on the tarp beside him and pulled myself under the truck. It must have been a while since I'd last played mechanic, because there wasn't nearly as much room under the truck as I remembered. I couldn't even get my arms up, let alone hold out the note, so I returned it to my pocket.

"It's a puzzle," I replied. "And I think it's serious."

"I'll take your word for it," he said as he strained to reach something at the edge of his fingertips. "Hey, could you hand me that bolt? I think I set it by your hip."

I felt around for the missing bolt, then dropped it into his hand. It might have been a while since I'd last squirmed under the truck, but at least our routine hadn't changed. That calmed me down a little. And if Toby wasn't worried, maybe I shouldn't be, either.

"Well, that's it," he said, giving the chassis a familiar pat. "This boat is almost ready to set sail." He sent me a sideways glance. "So Camp Vermeer or bust?"

I shook my head, then nodded. "Yeah, Camp Vermeer or bust."

But even I could tell that I didn't really mean it.

We dragged ourselves back to our feet, but it wasn't like we could just leave. They had a few more things to fix before the truck was good and ready, and I'd promised the director I wouldn't miss times table sprints.

Times table sprints were dumb (as usual), but Director Verity's workshop on rotational symmetry was kind of cool. We even got to go outside and look for examples in nature. Whistler was the only one who found one (though his pale pink evening primrose wasn't *technically* symmetrical, since it was missing one of its petals), but it was nice to be outside. Birds were chirping, bees were buzzing, and for the first time in a long time, the sun was actually shining. Then Director Verity had to go and ruin it. We'd just reached the amphitheater, a terraced semicircle with split logs and a fire pit, when she announced that it was time for us to head back to the lodge.

I felt my shoulders sag. "Can't we stay a little longer?" I wasn't ready to go back to the not-so-great indoors.

"Unfortunately, no," Director Verity replied. "We don't have time for lollygagging."

I scowled despite myself. Oliver sent me a smug look, then followed Director Verity. I guess he still hadn't forgiven me for getting him in trouble. The rest of the math nerds seemed perfectly willing to obey, but I allowed myself to dawdle, weaving in and out of the log benches, tracing the wood grain with both hands. I was just starting to enjoy myself when I found another clue:

```
Unicorn's nickname begins with the same
letter as Manticore's first name.
```

It had been folded twice and tucked into the deepest split, but I'd recognized the paper. I crouched down instinctively and surveyed the surrounding countryside. Director Verity and the math nerds were stretched out in a line on their way back to the lodge, and below the amphitheater, Lake Wannacrunchanumber was glistening like a broken mirror. No one within ten miles was paying the least bit of attention to me.

No one except the killer.

I shoved the clue into my pocket, then dragged myself back to my feet. In my rush to get away, I banged my knee into a bench, but I didn't stop to baby it, just forced myself to hobble. There was only one person at this camp that I trusted without question, and that was Toby. He might have ignored me before, but he couldn't ignore another clue. I would *make* him understand.

I must have been hobbling a lot slower than I'd thought, because the math nerds were already out of sight by the time I rounded the bend. When I burst into the lodge, I didn't stop to catch my breath, just barreled toward the stairs.

Ms. Gutierrez was grading worksheets, but she only had to take one look at me before she set her green pen down.

"Is something wrong?" she asked.

I didn't bother to slow down. "I just need to speak to Toby."

Ms. Gutierrez hurried to catch up. "I'm sorry, Esther," she replied, "but that won't be possible."

She managed to catch hold of my sleeve, but I ripped it out of her grasp.

"Why not?"

Ms. Gutierrez blinked. "Because he's gone," she said simply.

CHAPTER 14

The air rushed out of my lungs. It was like when Betsy Walker accidentally kneed me in the stomach in the middle of a bout.

Except it was ten times worse.

"What do you mean? He can't be *gone.* His rusty truck is right outside."

"Oh, he's not *gone* gone," she replied (though she wouldn't meet my eyes). "He just ran down to Morgan to pick up something for the truck. Mr. Pearson had to make a trip, so he offered him a ride." She pulled her phone out of her pocket. "They should be back by noon or so."

"They should be back by noon?" I asked as I pulled out my own phone. It was just after eleven.

"Or so," she said vaguely, putting an arm around my shoulders. "In the meantime, why don't you get changed? We're on our way down to the lake."

She was clearly trying to distract me, but I let her steer me toward the stairs, wiggling out of her grip when Mr. Sharp distracted *her*. Somehow, he'd sidled up to her without either of us noticing, and when she stopped to tweak his nose, I hightailed it out of there. She was clearly hiding something, too, and it probably had to do with Toby. If I was quick about it, I could look around for clues.

But the stairs were crammed with math nerds with alarmingly bare chests. Federico's swimsuit was practically scraping his ankles, but Graham's and Marshane's trunks didn't even come down to their knees. I couldn't even glance at Oliver's bright orange Speedo.

"Hey, Esther," Munch said brightly.

"Hey, Munch," I replied. At least he was wearing a T-shirt.

"Are you coming with us to the lake?"

"That's the plan," I said. "But I'll have to catch up to you guys." Under my breath, I added, "There have been some new developments."

I jumped the final steps, then darted up the corridor. At least Cabin Epsilon was empty. I pulled out my sketchbook and added the new clue to the list:

1. Satyr and Minotaur share a cabin with two other monsters.
2. Siren has a nickname.

3. Hydra and Cyclops are involved in a not-so-secret fling.
4. Centaur, Griffin, Unicorn, and Manticore share a cabin.
5. Phoenix wears glasses.
6. Unicorn's nickname begins with the same letter as Manticore's first name.

I stared. I glared. And I got nothing.

Sighing, I shucked off my clothes and wriggled into the blue swimsuit I hadn't planned on wearing. I'd grown a few inches since last summer, and Mom still hadn't replaced it. I checked myself out in the mirror, then yanked my shirt back on, returned my sketchbook to my pillowcase, and hurried out the door.

My feet thumped in time with my own heart as I raced back down the hall. I tried Cabin Beta first, but someone had locked the door. I thought about knocking, then changed my mind at the last second. Next, I checked the living areas—the mess hall, the game room, the sitting room, and the theater— but there were no clues to be found.

On my way to the common room, I snuck past the director's office—and couldn't help but notice that the thick door was ajar. She must have been distracted and forgotten to close it.

Maybe she'd been distracted by a certain someone's stepdad.

After tapping on the door, I toed it open wide enough to slither through sideways, then softly clicked it shut behind me. The office was as boring as it was predictable: brown paneling, huge bookcases, lots of charts and graphs. An old-fashioned radio sat on the corner of the desk next to a blindingly bright sunlamp. But no amount of sunshine, counterfeit or otherwise, was going to revive her shriveled plant, which might have been a daisy back when it was getting water.

I eyed that plant for a long moment, then turned my attention to the desk. I wasn't sure what I was looking for, but I had to believe that I would know it when I saw it. Unfortunately, the director's desk was as barren as a desert wasteland, without a paper clip or even a speck of lint in sight.

I tiptoed over to the door and pressed my ear against the seam, then, when I didn't hear anyone coming, crept back over to the desk and lowered myself into the chair. Either the director didn't keep anything important in her desk, or she was more trusting than she looked, because none of the drawers were locked. But the folders were so full there was no way they'd surrender their secrets without a fight.

Sighing, I tried the last drawer, the skinny one in the middle. It was crammed with odds and ends, but everything was in its place, with pens and pencils on one side and coins and thumbtacks on the other. The only thing that looked even remotely out of place was a partially torn check.

A check with Toby's signature.

I seized it without thinking, then yelped and dropped it on the desk (so as not to smudge the fingerprints). The check had been made out to Director Verity for a cool six hundred dollars.

I leaned back in my seat. Was this hush money of some sort? Had Toby tried to pay her off? But if that was the case, wouldn't *she* have paid *him* off? I was still trying to sort out what I thought the check could mean when footsteps padded down the hall. Someone was right outside the door.

I pinched the check between two fingers, slipped it back into the drawer, and eased the drawer shut with both hands, praying that the rollers wouldn't squeak. Then I crouched down behind the door. The footsteps had moved off, but whoever they'd belonged to probably wasn't out of sight.

I counted to ninety, then pressed my other ear against the seam. If Director Verity caught me, there was no telling what she'd do. After drawing a deep breath, I carefully cracked open the door and tiptoed out into the hall. I'd just crept across the common room when I bumped into Mr. Pearson, who was drooping awkwardly beneath the weight of a large package draped with an old, ratty towel.

"Watch it!" Mr. Pearson blurted as he spun away from me.

I couldn't help but grin. "You're back!"

"As you can see," was all he said. He shielded the package with his body.

I strained to see over his shoulder. "Has Toby come in yet?"

Mr. Pearson shook his head. "Mr. Renfro stayed in town."

I felt my shoulders fall. "He w*hat*?"

"There was a piece of twisted metal that he needed for his truck, so he said he'd wait for it." Mr. Pearson's nostrils flared. "Now, if you'll excuse me, I need to get started on lunch."

With one last harrumph, he continued on his way. My head was buzzing with so many questions that I just stood there, stunned. Why had Toby stayed in town? Even if he'd needed a used part, wouldn't he have also needed a way to get back up the mountain? He wouldn't have just left me here—unless someone had made him leave.

We spent the whole afternoon gathering data at the lake. Mr. Pearson even brought us lunch so we wouldn't have to take a break. I kept checking the time and coming up with dumb excuses to find my way back to the lodge, but as it turned out, Ms. Gutierrez was even more stubborn than I was. She refused to leave until we finished all her drills and carefully recorded our results.

By the time we got back from the lake, I was a basket case. I'd spent most of the hike telling myself that everything was fine, that Toby wasn't really gone, that he'd know what to do about the killer and these clues. But when we rounded the last corner, the very first thing I noticed was that the camp's cherry-red truck was the only one in sight.

I stopped dead in my tracks. "Toby's truck," I said. "Where is it?"

Ms. Gutierrez blinked. "Maybe he took it for a test drive?"

"No, Mr. Pearson said that he left Toby in town."

"Well, then, maybe he came back and got it. He must have wanted to make sure it was completely operational before you two, uh, left."

She couldn't have sounded more suspicious if she'd confessed to killing him. She tried to take hold of my arm, but I jerked it out of her grip.

"How did he get up the mountain? It isn't like he could have walked."

Ms. Gutierrez held her hands up. "Esther, I'm positive there's a perfectly rational explanation—"

"Then I want to talk to him," I said. "And I want to talk to him right now."

She glanced at Mr. Sharp, who pushed his glasses up his nose. The math nerds shifted anxiously, but I held my ground. If they wouldn't let me *talk* to Toby, I was going to assume that everyone was in on it. That they were all mass murderers.

Before Ms. Gutierrez had a chance to declare herself, the heavy oak door opened, and Director Verity appeared. Her gaze bounced back and forth between the counselors and me. "What's going on?" she asked.

I stuck out my chin. "I said, I want to talk to Toby." When the director arched an eyebrow, I stuck my chin back in and peeped, "If it isn't too much trouble."

She pressed her lips into a line, and for a second, I was sure that she was going to say no. I started hatching plots to break back into her office and steal her precious satellite phone, but she managed to surprise me.

"Come on," she finally said, wrapping an arm around my shoulders. "Let's go and make that call."

She steered me through the door, across the dusty common room, and into her dreaded office. The sunlamp was still on, but now the radio was, too. It took my brain too many seconds to translate the noises into words.

"—for the next forgery to surface," the woman on the radio was saying, "but the so-called Fenimore Forger is keeping a low profile at present."

The radio clicked off. "Have a seat," Director Verity said.

Obediently, I had a seat. I would have liked to hear the rest, but letting myself get riled up about the Fenimore Forger wasn't going to help me locate Toby.

She sat down in her chair and offered me her satellite phone. If I hadn't known what it was, I probably would have thought it was some kind of walkie-talkie with a super-thick antenna. It looked solid enough to bludgeon someone with.

"If you don't want to go outside, you'll have to stand over by the window"—she flicked a thumb over her shoulder—"and angle the antenna toward the sky."

I probably should have jumped at the chance to put some space between us, and yet I stayed right where she was. If she'd had something to do with Toby's sudden disappearance, she surely would have guessed that I would want some privacy, but if she'd also guessed that I would guess what she'd just guessed, didn't that undo the guessing? Instead of playing her mind games, I held the phone up to my ear, but it was as dead as her daisy.

"Oh, I must have forgotten the SIM card."

How convenient, I was about to say, then caught myself at the last second.

She snatched the phone out of my hands, produced a small chip out of nowhere, and snapped the chip into the phone. When the blue screen glowed to life, she passed the whole thing back to me. "Now you have to dial two zeroes and a one, plus the number you want to call."

I dialed two zeroes and a one, then glanced at Director Verity. She was pretending to flip through a magazine, but from the way her eyes were skipping back and forth across the pages, I could tell that she was watching. When two of her pages stuck together, I quickly punched in Toby's number.

"Don't you have something to do?"

"Nothing that can't be done later," she said. "This phone can be tricky."

The phone wasn't the only thing that could be tricky.

It kept ringing and ringing. I kept my eyes glued to the window, hoping she would take the hint, but she kept flipping through her magazine (which was thicker than most books). She did look up once or twice, but when her gaze landed on the picture on the corner of her desk, she sent me a sideways glance, then calmly turned it upside down. My fingers itched to flip it over, but I couldn't muster the courage before the call went to his voicemail.

I didn't bother to leave a message. It seemed like a waste of time. But just because he hadn't answered didn't mean he *couldn't* answer. Toby had never been much of a phone picker-upper.

Or at least that was what I told myself.

Director Verity looked up. "Unavailable?" she asked.

I forced myself to nod. "Can I try my mom instead?"

The director cleared her throat. "You know, it's *possible* that everything's worked out precisely as it was supposed to. Maybe you were meant to come—and maybe now you're meant to stay." She leaned forward in her seat. "Do you understand, Esther?"

Goose bumps crawled up and down my arms, but I forced myself not to rub them. I wanted her to think I had absolutely no idea what she was referring to. "I just want to call my mom."

Director Verity leaned back. "If that's what you really want," she said.

I punched in Mom's number, then punched it in again after two zeroes and a one. This time, it only rang twice before it kicked me to her voicemail.

"Hey, Mom," I said after it beeped. "Everything's great, everything's fine—nothing weird is going on—but I wanted to check in and see how things were there at home. You haven't come across *Westinghouse's Resting Place*, have you?" *Westinghouse's Resting Place* was one of Toby's works-in-progress, a deconstructed microwave designed to look like a graveyard, but he'd been stuck on it for months. I couldn't tell Mom what was happening with the director listening in, but hopefully, that would tip her off. "Well, I should probably let you go. My phone doesn't work up here, but if you need to get in touch, you can reach me at this number. *It's Director Verity's.*" Under my breath, I added, "Love you."

We weren't a touchy-feely family, but chasing homicidal maniacs put things in perspective.

After wiping off the grease that my cheek had left behind, I handed her the phone again. She didn't bother to pretend that she hadn't been eavesdropping, just returned it to her desk.

"Did you need anything else?"

I needed lots of things—answers, Toby, Angeline—but since I strongly suspected she knew more than she was saying, I just frowned and shook my head.

Time for another secret meeting.

CHAPTER 15

The clock on my phone had just flipped to 7:12 when Marshane got up and stretched, drained his root beer in one swallow, and announced he had to pee. He'd been nursing the root beer since dinner so this announcement would sound plausible. The last thing we wanted to do was give away our careful plan.

We'd spaced out our departures by two minutes and twelve seconds—twelve was Marshane's favorite number—so we wouldn't look suspicious, but the other people in the game room probably couldn't have cared less. Whistler and a kid who never spoke were playing some kind of board game, Brooklyn was reading in the corner, and Mr. Sharp and Ms. Gutierrez were too busy playing footsie with each other to pay attention to their charges. Still, Marshane didn't look at me as he sauntered toward the bathroom, and two minutes and twelve seconds later, I sauntered after him.

Anxiety forced me to hurry as soon as I was out of sight. I'd been the last person to leave, so everyone would be waiting for me. As I dashed into the common room, I glanced over my shoulder to see if I was being followed and crashed into Mr. Pearson for the second time that day.

As we bounced off each other, I immediately dropped my gaze and mumbled, "I guess I didn't see you there."

Mr. Pearson's nostrils flared. "I believe you meant to say you didn't see me there *again*."

I didn't bother to reply, but he didn't let me off the hook.

"Where were you going?" he demanded, folding his arms across his chest. There was a tattoo on his forearm that looked a lot like a Rembrandt, but I doubted that it was. As discreetly as I could, I craned my neck to check it out, but then he noticed me noticing and unfolded his arms.

"Where was I going?" I replied, then wished I could take it back. Could that have sounded any more suspicious? I cleared my throat and tried again: "I mean, I'm going to the bathroom."

Mr. Pearson's eyes narrowed. "Why didn't you use the one in the mess hall?"

I willed my voice not to crack. "Someone was using it," I said.

He didn't blink. "I see." When I just stood there breathing, he flicked a thumb over his shoulder. "Well, then, go to the bathroom."

With a sharp dip of my head, I went swiftly on my way. I expected him to go on his, but he just stood there waiting. Watching. At least the door wasn't locked.

I hadn't planned to turn the light on, but since Mr. Pearson was still watching I had to look and act normal. The lights clawed at my eyes as I shut the door behind me and squinted at myself in the mirror. I looked paler than I usually did, less confident, more scared. I wrapped my hands around the sink and waited for my pulse to slow.

According to Ms. Gutierrez, Mr. Pearson was the last person who'd seen Toby alive.

But I couldn't dwell on that. I couldn't prove anything (yet), and I had a meeting to get to. After giving Mr. Pearson plenty of time to go about his business, I flipped off the lights and gently pried open the window. The air felt cold on my face, and I realized I was sweating—on my forehead, under my arms, and in certain other places that we didn't need to mention.

After drying off my hands, I hoisted myself out of the window. Tree bark crunched under my feet as I crept along the wall, loud enough to make me wince. I kept waiting for Director Verity to hear me from her room and step out onto her balcony, but she never appeared. When I reached the storage room, I tapped on the window once, then twice, then three times to let them know that it was me, then let myself in.

The storage room felt emptier. Graham was slumped against one stack of boxes, and Marshane was sitting on another. Munch was digging through a pouch in the corner by the easel. When he found an old package of Runts, he popped one into his mouth.

As soon as I dropped to the floor, Graham scrambled to his feet. "Oliver said he couldn't make it."

Marshane didn't get up. "*Actually*, he said, 'I think Esther's a psycho, but if you guys want to hang out with her, you're more than welcome to.' "

Graham glared at Marshane, but I couldn't have cared less.

"Oliver can say anything he wants as long as he doesn't interfere." I glanced down at Munch, who was still digging through his pouch. "I assume those are the lock picks?"

Munch gave his pouch a pat. "What's a picklock without his tools?"

Marshane cocked an eyebrow. "Do you always answer questions by asking another question?"

Munch's nose crinkled. "Do you always act like such a punk?"

Marshane's grin swallowed his face.

"Come on, guys," I said, sighing. "We're never gonna find them if we keep fighting among ourselves."

Graham scratched the back of his head. "What if they're not out there to find? What if they really did go home?"

"They couldn't have gone home," I replied. "Toby's truck vanished *after* he disappeared, and Angeline left her stuff behind."

He opened his mouth to answer, then swiftly snapped it shut again.

I forced myself not to smirk. He couldn't argue with my logic. "My plan has two parts," I went on as I pulled out my sketchbook. I'd passed the time in the game room sketching the math nerds as Greek monsters, so I kept that part covered. "The first part is pretty easy—I just need you guys to keep an eye out for more clues. If you find one, get it to me as quickly as you can so we can add it to the log."

"Oh, that reminds me," Marshane said as he produced a scrap of paper. "I found this one in the potted palm outside the theater."

```
Cyclops and Chimera share a cabin with
no other monsters.
```

Graham's eyes narrowed threateningly. "What were you doing in the theater?"

"*Relaxing*," he replied.

I fought the urge to roll my eyes. How Marshane spent his free time was up to him, not up to me, but it would have been nice if he'd told me about the clue. "And you were gonna tell us when?"

He considered that, then shrugged. "Right now?"

"Fine," I said waspishly as I crammed it into my sketchbook. I tried to remember where I was. "But the second part involves busting into Archimedes's shed."

Munch's eyes glowed. "*Yes.*"

Marshane raised his hand. "I don't mind breaking or entering, but why go to all the trouble? Why not just focus on the clues?"

"The clues are our fail-safe, but I don't want to let the killer decide our next moves for us." I let my eyes drift toward the hill. "We've got to take him by surprise."

They didn't even try to argue.

I met their gazes one by one. "Part one will go into effect as soon as we leave this room, but we'll leave part two until tonight."

Marshane snorted obnoxiously. "Because that worked out so well last time."

I chucked my pencil at his head. "Last time, Brooklyn sold us out, but she won't interfere tonight."

"How do you know?" Marshane demanded.

I sent him a secret smile. "Because I know how to push her buttons."

CHAPTER 16

We launched Operation Pepto-Bismol at dinner that evening. After lunch's lettuce wraps, I was worried we'd be having something troublesome like salad, but we were having sloppy joes. I forced myself not to grin as I slumped into the line. If there was one medium any prank artist could work with, it was a scoop of sloppy joe.

After asking Mr. Sharp for an extra scoop or two, I grabbed the seat closest to Brooklyn. I tried to make it look like I wasn't thinking straight, but whatever I was selling, Brooklyn wasn't buying it.

"I think you're lost," she grumbled, motioning toward Munch and Graham. "Why don't you go and sit with them?"

"I don't know," I said. "I just thought it would be nice if we could have a girls' night in."

"What are we going to do, paint each other's nails?" she asked.

I gulped. "Yeah, sure," I said. If I was going to convince her, then I couldn't flake out.

Brooklyn rolled her eyes. "I don't paint my nails, dimwit, and I don't want to paint yours, either."

But I wasn't deterred. Instead of backing off, I scooted closer. "If you don't want to paint our nails, we could have an eating contest." I'd already chugged a chocolate milk, so my breath was nice and ripe. "I spent the afternoon holed up in the bathroom, but I'm feeling better now."

Brooklyn's nose crinkled. "Good for you," she said as she scooted farther down the bench, but it sounded more like, *Stay away from me, sicko.*

"Yeah, good for me," I said, taking a bite of sloppy joe. A glob of sauce dribbled down my chin, leaving a trail of greasy ooze. When Brooklyn noticeably shuddered, I had to duck my head so she wouldn't see my smile. You really couldn't script these things.

I inhaled my sloppy joe—or at least I pretended to. No sooner had I taken my fifth bite than Munch started sneezing. Violently. While Brooklyn's attention was on him, I wrapped up my sloppy joe and tucked it into my pocket, then drew her attention back to me by massaging my stomach.

"Oh, man," I said, groaning. "Maybe I shouldn't have pushed it."

At first, Brooklyn didn't answer, and I flinched despite myself. I must have laid it on too thick. Somehow, she'd guessed that I was playing her; now she was playing me. But then she covered her mouth, and I knew I'd gotten to her.

It was time to move on to phase two.

"Watch my French fries," I added as I lurched out of my seat and made a beeline for the bathroom. When I slammed the door shut on my heels, I caught the corner with my toe so it couldn't close completely. If I was going to get Brooklyn to buy my Kool-Aid after all, she couldn't miss the grand finale.

While the door was mostly closed, I pulled my treasures from my pockets: my leftover sloppy joe and my mostly empty chocolate milk. My cargo pants were going to smell like leftover Italian for a week, but that was a small price to pay for Operation Pepto-Bismol. After making sure that Brooklyn didn't have a line of sight, I ripped open the carton, jammed the sloppy joe into the opening, and stirred the whole thing with my finger. Those last few drops of chocolate milk were going to make it extra creamy.

Once I'd put the final touches on my gloopy, soupy mess, I got down on my hands and knees and cozied up to the toilet. This part was going to be tricky. I had to make it look like I was barfing without actually barfing. And I had to do it for an audience.

Clutching the carton in the hand that was closest to the

wall, I tucked my elbow by my side, then nudged the door open with my toe. While I pretended to gag, I shook my concoction into the toilet. A few globs even missed the bowl and splattered all over the rim. Jackson Pollock himself couldn't have done a better job.

I had no way of knowing if Brooklyn was seeing my performance, but then, the other math nerds *were* whooping and hollering like monkeys. Once I'd emptied the carton, I faked one final convulsion and kicked the door shut all the way. I couldn't flush the carton, but with any luck, Brooklyn would be so grossed out she wouldn't bother to investigate. I buried it under a handful of used tissues, then hopped back to my feet.

As I washed off my hands and face, I inspected myself in the mirror. I hadn't brushed my hair since yesterday, so it looked suitably mussed. My cheeks were probably too bright, but hopefully, if Brooklyn noticed, she'd just think I was feverish.

When I finally crawled out of the bathroom, Brooklyn was scowling at her tray, and Marshane was snickering. He probably would have snickered even if I'd really been sick, but I didn't look at him for fear of snickering myself. Luckily, Director Verity was paying him no heed.

I glanced back at the bathroom. "Sorry about the mess," I mumbled. "I guess I'm still feeling sick."

Director Verity made a face. "You've had a long day," she replied. "Why don't you just go to bed?"

I nodded miserably, but when Brooklyn didn't say a word, my heart started to pound. If she didn't take the bait, we were going to have to call off the whole mission. I sent Graham a sideways glance, but he just shook his head. He didn't know what to do, either.

Since I was fresh out of ideas, I staggered toward the stairs. I'd just grabbed hold of the railing when Brooklyn leaped out of her seat.

"I'd like to request a change of rooms!"

I paused on the landing, trying not to look too hopeful.

Director Verity pursed her lips, then, finally, sighed. "Very well," she said. "You may sleep in Cabin Zeta for tonight—but *only* for tonight."

As I dragged myself up the stairs, I couldn't help but risk a tiny grin. Operation Houdini was up next.

CHAPTER 17

Cabin Epsilon was quiet—Munch would probably say too quiet—as I waited for the hours to pass. With no roommate to hoodwink, I huddled on my bunk fully clothed and flicked my flashlight on and off. Not even my sketchbook had been able to distract me. It was like I knew my time was coming.

Finally, at 10:16, I eased my sliding door open and tip-toed out onto the balcony. An owl hooted eerily as I lowered myself over the edge, and it was all that I could do not to curl up into a ball. After reminding myself that I did *not* believe in ghosts (just real, live mass murderers who were probably too smart to give themselves away by hooting), I snaked around the flower beds and cut across the gravel driveway, dodging patches of moonlight. I didn't plan to use my flash-light until we were in the shed.

By the time I reached the narrow road that wound up to

Archimedes's cabin, I could already see the shapes of the math nerds waiting for me. When Federico turned his head into a shaft of silver moonlight, the smudges under his dark eyes immediately captured my attention.

"Nice makeup," I said, smiling.

"It's not *makeup*, it's eye black. It's supposed to make me look more threatening."

He'd joined our motley crew after discovering a clue under the pool table in the game room: *Harpy is a girl*. Thankfully, he'd shown it to Graham instead of Director Verity. We'd only exchanged a dozen words, but I'd already figured out he was the opposite of threatening. Still, because he'd made himself such a straightforward punch line, I couldn't bring myself to actually say it out loud.

"Are you ready?" I asked Munch instead.

He held up his trusty pouch. "Are *you*?"

I forced myself not to grin. Marshane had definitely pinned him, but teasing Munch about his tendency to answer questions with more questions was only going to make him more uptight, and we desperately needed him to focus.

I surveyed my motley crew. I really only needed Munch, but Graham, Marshane, and Federico had also decided to show up. If they thought this would be a nature hike, they were in for a surprise.

"Oh!" Munch said suddenly, plunging a hand into his pocket. "I found another clue."

He handed it to me, but I couldn't read it in the dark.

"What does it say?" I asked.

" 'Minotaur's first name begins with the same letter as Hydra's last name.' I committed it to memory."

I slid the clue into my pocket. "All right, let's go," I said. "The sooner we get in, the sooner we can get back out."

I headed up the hill like a bloodhound on the scent, the other math nerds on my heels. We only made it a few feet before I noticed a low growl emanating from somewhere behind us. The hairs on the back of my neck prickled as I visualized a grizzly bear stalking through the undergrowth. I raised a fist to call a halt, but whatever was growling halted, too. My pulse fluttered wildly—until I realized our grizzly bear was a mouth-breathing Marshane.

"If you can't close that yap," I said, "I'm gonna have to send you packing."

"Hey, it's not my fault," he hissed. "My dumb foot fell asleep while we were waiting for Eye Black, and now it's starting to tingle."

"Well, then, make it *stop* tingling. If our old friend Archimedes decides to pull out his shotgun, you're gonna want to be able to run."

I could almost hear the blood draining out of Marshane's cheeks. "Archimedes has a shotgun?"

"Theoretically," I said. "But he's not gonna pull it out because he's not gonna see us."

The others nodded nervously, and we went back to hiking. We only made it three feet, though, before someone cursed under his breath.

I stopped again. "Now what?"

"It's my eye black," Federico said. "I think I smeared it in my eye!"

"Why were you touching it?" I asked.

"You're not supposed to touch it?" he replied.

I fought the urge to smack my forehead.

Graham was more generous. "Have you ever used eye black before?"

"In real life?" he asked. "Well, no. Coach never puts me in. But I *have* tried it on in front of the mirror lots of times."

This time, I didn't fight the urge.

"Here," Graham said gallantly. I couldn't see what he passed him, but it sounded like a water bottle. "You can rinse it off with this."

Marshane shook his head. "That's not gonna work," he said. "Eye black won't mix with water. If he wants to get it off, he'll have to wipe it on his shirt."

"He can't wipe it on his shirt," I said. "Director Verity might see."

Munch ripped a clump of leaves off the nearest waist-high bush and offered it to Federico.

Federico took the clump. "What if it's poison ivy?"

Munch considered that, then shrugged. "There's only one way to find out."

Federico hesitated for another couple of seconds, then bravely wiped off his face. Once he could see again, we resumed our uphill climb. This time, we made it ten whole yards before something thumped behind me.

I whirled around. *"Now* what?"

Munch's shoulders hunched. "I accidentally dropped my tool kit."

Marshane flashed his teeth. They looked like tombstones in the dark. "At least you didn't ask a question."

Munch clenched his pudgy fists, but I threw myself between them before he had a chance to use them. For a bunch of brilliant math nerds, they could sometimes be meatheads.

"Spread out and find that pouch," I hissed. "We're kind of on a schedule here."

"We are?" Federico asked.

The truth was, we really weren't—as long as we were back by morning, no one would notice we'd snuck out—but Mom always brought up schedules when I was being difficult. "No more questions," I replied, "or I'll send all of you home!"

At least that shut them up. We got down on our hands and knees and felt around for Munch's pouch. The ground was cold and lumpy; I tried not to think too hard about what those lumps might be. At least it only took a minute for Graham to stumble across it.

Munch slipped it into his coat. "I guess I do have butterfingers."

"You do *not* have butterfingers. You have the most useful fingers in this whole camp, you understand?" I gave his back an awkward pat. "No more interruptions, though, okay? Let's just get in and get out."

The math nerds nodded gladly, and for once, they kept their word. We didn't have to stop again until we made it to the clearing. When I crouched down behind a bush vaguely shaped like a cauldron, the others hunkered down beside me.

"All right, here's the plan," I said. "I'm gonna infiltrate the shed, Munch and Graham are gonna watch my back, and Marshane and Federico are gonna keep an eye on theirs."

Federico nodded gamely, but Marshane wasn't convinced.

"Why are you taking Graham?" he asked. "He won't be much help in a fight."

Graham's nostrils shriveled into slits, but before he could defend himself, I held up a hand.

"For one thing," I replied, "there's not gonna be a fight, so it doesn't really matter. And for another, if there *is* a fight, someone needs to take care of Federico."

Federico's eye black sagged. "But I thought you just said—"

"Forget what I just said, all right?" I should have known to keep it simple. "In and out, remember? We'll be back before you know it."

Federico didn't look convinced, but he nodded, anyway. I thanked my lucky stars. I could deal with butterfingers and smeared eye black, but I drew the line at temper tantrums.

I signaled Munch and Graham to follow me. "Let's go."

I ducked under the bush and army-crawled out into the clearing, ignoring the pesky stickers that dug into my fleshy forearms. Thankfully, Munch and Graham seemed to be ignoring them, too. When I popped up in the grass, they popped up right behind me.

We took the same path around the cabin, scurrying across the road, then crouching down beside the ring of dirt. The grass got tangled in my hair, but I batted it away and concentrated on our goal. The shed was the key to this whole puzzle—I could feel it in my fingertips—and we were on the verge of cracking it.

We left Graham at the corner so he could cover our flank (a word I'd learned from Toby, which made my heart twist a little), then darted around the next corner and skidded to a halt. The shed squatted in the grass like a mud-encrusted troll. The padlock gleamed in the moonlight, practically begging to be picked.

"I'll cover you," I whispered, scanning this side of the clearing while Munch unpacked his tools. The grass swayed hypnotically in the cool mountain breeze, but I didn't let it get to me. If I let my guard down for even a fraction of a second, I might never see Toby or Angeline again.

The clanking of a heavy chain drew my attention back to the shed. Munch was kneeling by the doors, fiddling with the padlock. The tools he'd already tried were lying in a useless heap while the ones he hadn't tried yet were quickly dwindling to zero.

I squatted down beside him. "How's it going?" I whispered. It was pretty clear how it was going, but it seemed rude to point that out.

Munch gritted his teeth. "Not so well," he admitted.

My pulse pounded in my ears. "I thought you said you could crack it."

"I *can*," he said grumpily as he pulled a pair of bolt cutters out from under his shirt.

"Where have you been hiding *those*?" I asked. They were a foot long and had to weigh as much as my left leg.

"They're Mr. Pearson's," he replied as he got into position. "I just asked if I could borrow them." He motioned toward the doors. "Now get over here and help."

I wiped my hands off on my jeans. "What if Archimedes hears us?"

Munch waved that away. "Do you want to get into this shed or not?"

At least he was back to answering questions with more questions.

I drew a shallow breath, then took hold of the other handle. It felt warm in my hands, but it felt solid, too, like it could shatter bones as easily as it could shatter chains. Maybe that was why my conscience picked that moment to attack me. We were literally breaking and entering—and we probably weren't done. But what about Angeline and Toby? Weren't they more than worth the risk?

"Esther?" Munch whispered. "Are we doing this or not?"

I tightened my grip on the handle. "Oh, we're doing it," I said as I clenched my teeth and squeezed.

It took us several tries, but we finally managed to snap the heavy chain in half. The padlock swung back and forth like a shiny pendulum.

"Here," Munch said curtly, shoving the bolt cutters into my hands. I had no choice but to take them as he unthreaded the chain. The clanking sounded too loud, but neither Archimedes nor his shotgun made an impromptu appearance. When Munch dropped the padlock at my feet, the doors swung slightly inward, like they were welcoming me home.

We'd made it into the shed.

The inside of the shed was as dark as a black hole. I could make out blocky shapes, but they could have been almost anything. Cabinets. Wheelbarrows. Hacksaws. Maybe Archimedes was a very special kind of sculptor.

Munch squinted into the gloom. "Now what?"

"Now," I said courageously as I pulled out my flashlight, "we lock ourselves in."

"We can't lock the doors from the inside. And even if we could, we snapped the chains in half, remember?"

I hadn't planned this far ahead. Time to make something up. "Then you can lock me in—or at least make it look like I'm locked in. Once you've got the doors secured, you can hide behind that bush and keep an eye out for Archimedes."

Munch shook his head. "Anyone who takes a good look at those chains will be able to tell that they've been cut."

"Then we'll have to hope that he's nearsighted. I haven't come this far to quit."

Munch held up his hands. "All right, all right, I'll do it, but only if you stop talking in cat posters."

I grinned despite myself and tightened my grip on my flashlight. "I'll let you know once I'm finished."

"If I don't hear from you in, like, five minutes, I'm coming in to get you."

I waited for Munch to close the doors, then flicked my flashlight on. After blinking the spots out of my eyes, I took a look around. At first, the shed's contents didn't seem out of the ordinary. There was a workbench, a broken rocking chair, and an upside-down green bike dangling from a pair of hooks. When I shone the flashlight down the workbench, the first thing I spotted was a stack of dusty textbooks. But the *second* thing I spotted was an old-fashioned typewriter.

It was a fancy-looking thing, with four dozen circle

buttons and a polished black roller. I would have bet dollars to doughnuts that it belonged to the killer.

I set the flashlight down so it would illuminate the workbench, then picked up the typewriter and carefully turned it over. I didn't know what to expect (though a PROPERTY OF DIRECTOR VERITY, RESIDENT MASS MURDERER label would have been nice), but the typewriter was clean, no fingerprints or scratches.

I got down on my hands and knees and shone my flashlight under the workbench, but except for a few stacks of brittle, yellowing newspapers, the space was also clean. Pushing my annoyance aside, I stood up again and ventured deeper into the shed. When I (literally) stumbled across a bookcase, I felt my pulse speed up. According to Ms. Clementi, my old journalism teacher, you could tell a lot about a person by the sorts of books he read, but except for the stash of romance novels, the books didn't tell me much.

Then I noticed that several of the spaces on the lowest shelf weren't dusty; someone must have just removed those books. Before that thought had finished forming, I dashed back over to the workbench to check the dusty textbooks' spines: *Introduction to Logic*, *A Concise Introduction to Logic*, and a dog-eared paperback called, appropriately, *The Game of Logic*. I was reaching for that last one when my gaze happened to land on a blond bobby pin.

Adrenaline surged through my veins as my fingers closed

around it. I didn't mess with bobby pins, blond or otherwise, and I was willing to bet that Brooklyn didn't, either.

It definitely proved there was a link between Angeline and the killer.

I stuffed the bobby pin into my pocket—after all, it wasn't stealing if you were simply taking back what belonged to someone else—then pawed through the textbooks, searching for something, *anything*, that would give me a hint as to what to do with all the clues. But despite its title, *A Concise Introduction to Logic* hadn't been designed to be read in thirty seconds.

I was weighing the pros and cons of just taking it with me when a pebble bumped against the shed. My initial thought was that I'd imagined it, but when a second pebble glanced off the shed in the same spot, I knew I hadn't made it up. Someone was coming, and Munch was trying to warn me.

I darted toward the doors, but when I pressed my ear to the seam, I could already make out the *thuds* of someone's heavy footsteps. There was no way I could escape without getting spotted by the someone (who was probably the killer), which left me with just one option: hide.

CHAPTER 18

I should have been freaking out as I wedged myself into the gap between the rocking chair and the near wall. There were only two people on earth who might find their way into this shed—Archimedes and the mass murderer—and I wasn't keen on meeting either. Still, I felt strangely calm as I pulled my knees up to my chest. If it was my time to ske-daddle, at least I could rightly say that I'd crashed a killer math camp.

Something rattled the chain Munch had meticulously replaced. When it hit the ground with a dull *clank*, I drew a silent breath and pressed my face into my knees. The doors whooshed open with a *bang*, making the hairs on the back of my neck stand up. Thankfully, I'd never borrowed any of Angeline's body spray, so unless the human nose could detect a freshly showered twelve-year-old, my smell wouldn't compromise me.

My heart thumped wildly as a pair of boots clomped into the shed. I could see them through the gap between my thigh and my elbow. They were smaller than I'd thought they'd be, but that didn't mean anything. Who said serial killers had to have big feet?

For the first minute or two, the intruder just stood there breathing. I kept waiting for a hand to drag me up by my hair, but the black boots never moved. Either I hadn't been spotted, or the intruder was trying to get me to relax.

I tried to hold perfectly still, sucking long breaths through my nose, but it was dustier down here than it had been up above, and I could feel a sneeze coming on. I crinkled my nose and willed myself not to blow, but if the intruder didn't leave soon, I'd have no choice but to give myself away.

Finally, the intruder took a few hesitant steps—deeper into the shed. I pressed my knee against that sensitive spot above my upper lip, but before I could explode, my phone, which had been searching for a signal for days, let out a cheerful *ding*.

I couldn't decide which was more amazing, that my phone had decided to start working or that it had decided to start working *now.* I heard more than saw the intruder glance over his shoulder, but instead of waiting around to shake his hand, I chucked the rocking chair aside and burst out of the shed. Munch was nowhere in sight, so I dove into the grass, making a beeline for the trees.

The clearing was less even on this side of the cabin. Rocks rolled under my feet, and a ditch nearly toppled me, but I managed to keep my balance. My breath was coming out in short, hot bursts, and my chest felt like it was on fire, but I didn't slow down. The tree line was ten yards away. If I could just make it a little farther—

I couldn't finish that thought before I was tumbling to the ground, cutting a deep swath through the grass as I rolled end over end. I hadn't heard a gunshot, but maybe I'd been breathing too hard.

For a long time, I just lay there, listening to my heart pound in my ears. At least my phone had stopped dinging. I kept waiting for a sticky warmth to spread across my torso (or wherever I'd been shot), but the only thing I felt was a sore spot on my side, as if I'd just taken an illegal hit from a broadsword. But there was no one else in sight.

I was about to sit up straight when a voice hissed, "No, stay down! The dude's headed this way."

"Who's headed this way?" I asked, but the voice just shushed me.

Mom had always believed in guardian angels, and right then, I decided to believe in them, too. I curled up into a ball and pressed my cheek into the dirt, waiting for the killer to find me. But then a full minute passed, and no one finished me off. Finally, the voice said, "You're good. He went back the other way."

I pushed myself onto my knees, then crawled the last ten yards to the tree line, where I promptly flopped under a bush. It could have been poison ivy for all I cared. But when something rustled in the bush next to mine, my muscles tensed to spring.

"Relax," the same voice said. "It's just the Three Stooges and me."

I rolled onto my side, and there they were, Federico and Marshane, even Munch and Graham. Federico's eye black was a mess, and Graham's shirt had come untucked, but other than that, they looked all right. I tried to sit up, but the sore spot in my side, which suddenly hurt like Charles Dickens, didn't want me to move. The adrenaline must have been wearing off.

Marshane's cheeks actually darkened. "Sorry about the rock," he mumbled as he helped me to my feet. "I had to get you down somehow."

"That was *you*?" I asked, shining my flashlight in his face. "I thought I'd just been shot!"

Graham would have kept apologizing, but Marshane just grinned.

"I knew those pitching lessons would come in handy someday," he replied.

Munch shoved Marshane. "You didn't have to hit her!"

"Actually, I did." He tipped his head back toward the clearing. "It looked like the killer was about to turn the corner, and I didn't see you bozos coming up with any bright ideas."

Munch stuck out his chin. "I was gonna get her out."

"Well, you didn't," Marshane said.

"I sacrificed my Runts to save her!"

So they'd been Runts, not pebbles. I guess that made more sense.

"I got myself out, thanks," I said as I dusted off my hands. "So what else did you guys see?"

They exchanged uneasy looks. Finally, Federico said, "Not much. He was wearing a big coat."

"It hasn't been *that* chilly," I replied.

Federico shrugged. "Maybe he was hiding his identity."

"Or *her* identity," I grumbled.

Graham didn't bother to ask me what I meant. "So did you find anything?"

"A few things," I admitted, patting the bobby pin for good measure.

Munch wiped off his mouth. "Why'd you take off like a loose spring?"

"Because my phone rang," I replied, wrestling it out of my pocket. At least they couldn't see me wince.

Graham's forehead wrinkled. "Our phones don't work up here."

Marshane pulled his out of his pocket. "Maybe they work up *here*," he said.

While Graham surveyed the starry sky like he was worried it might fall on him, and Munch and Marshane debated the finer points of cell technology, I finally freed my phone.

The missed call was from Toby.

CHAPTER 19

I scrambled onto my knees, ignoring the pain in my side. Toby had tried to call me. Toby had *just* tried to call me.

I was still wrapping my brain around these facts when my phone dinged again. It caught me so off guard that I actually dropped it. With trembling hands, I scooped it up, flipped it open, and peeped, "Toby?"

Munch and Marshane stopped arguing. Federico tried to say something, but I waved him off. I couldn't hear a thing, not even static. Did that mean he was underground? But if he was underground, how had he called me in the first place?

"Toby?" I asked again. When he didn't answer right away, I feverishly scanned the screen. The voicemail icon was blinking. I felt myself slowly deflate.

Marshane jerked the phone out of my hands. "What's going on?" he asked.

Graham jerked it out of *his* hands. "Do you have *any* manners?"

"Come on, guys," Munch replied. "No more messing around. Esther's stepdad is missing."

Grudgingly, Graham plopped the phone back into my waiting hand. I jabbed the voicemail button and pressed the phone against my ear. A dozen feelings crowded me, but as soon as I heard Toby's voice, the one that cornered me was dread:

"Esther, I—got me—truck. You—need to worry—and *don't call home again.* You need to—yourself."

I listened to it one more time, but the message didn't change. Something—or some*one*—had gotten Toby, but I could no longer call home. The killer must have found out where we lived. I'd accidentally led him straight to Mom.

"Well?" Marshane demanded.

I didn't bother to reply, just pressed my phone into his hands. I was too freaked out to explain.

Marshane listened to the voicemail, then grimly passed the phone to Graham, who handed it to Federico, who finally passed it to Munch. Despite the terrible lighting, I could see the blood drain from his cheeks.

"That really stinks," Munch whispered as he passed it back to me.

Graham shook his head aggressively. "It doesn't have to mean he's captured. We couldn't hear, like, half the words."

Federico shook his, too. "We heard enough," was all he said.

I'd jumped to the same conclusion, but hearing him say it out loud made me want to plug my ears.

Munch lowered his gaze. "What are we gonna do now?"

I clenched my hands into fists. "We're gonna solve this stupid puzzle. Then we're gonna find our friends."

I didn't get much sleep that night, partly because we'd stayed out so late but mostly because I couldn't stop thinking about Toby's voicemail. When I woke up the next morning, I could feel the bags under my eyes from the inside of my face. Still, I clambered out of bed, unable or unwilling to give up. As of 11:10 last night, Toby had still been alive. I couldn't let myself lose hope.

It wasn't until I was halfway down the stairs that I remembered I should be careful. We'd done everything we could to cover our tracks the night before, but if the director had found out by some awful twist of fate, we were about to get busted.

I hesitated on the last step, bracing myself for an explosion, but the first thing I noticed when I entered the mess hall was that it was empty. Trays were scattered around tables, and the enormous vat of oatmeal that Mr. Pearson had been tending was no longer steaming. It felt like I'd crawled into a painting that was only halfway done.

I tightened my grip on the railing and was about to all-out scream when I spotted clumps of people milling around the common room. Director Verity's neat bun was looming near the front, and Mr. Sharp's shiny bald head was hovering off to the side. The rest of the math nerds were spread out in a line behind them.

"—is *that* supposed to mean?" Oliver was asking as I sidled up to him.

Munch considered that, then shrugged. "I think it looks like Belarusan *Wheel of Fortune*."

They were facing the chalkboards, one of which had been wiped clean in the middle of the night. The math nerds' calculations had been reduced to swirls of chalk; in their place was another puzzle:

BO YKU DJKW WaFT'S RKKi OKQ YKU,
TaMJ YKU'GG STFY KUT KO HY WKQDQKKH

Someone had printed off each letter on its own piece of paper, kind of like a ransom note made of cut-up magazines. But the last time I checked, "BO YKU DJKW WAFT'S RKKI OKQ YKU, TAMJ YKU'GG STFY KUT KO HY WKQDQKKH" didn't spell anything.

I gritted my teeth. This had the work of a mass murderer written all over it. While we'd been infiltrating his lair, he'd been infiltrating ours.

I must have been making a face, because Graham arched an eyebrow at me. *Are you thinking what I'm thinking?* that eyebrow seemed to ask.

Carefully, I shook my head. Unless Graham was fantasizing about dueling our killer, we weren't thinking the same thing.

The director cleared her throat. "Well, number crunchers," she said strangely, "it looks like *someone* has treated us to a substitution cipher."

"By erasing my work," Brooklyn grumbled. "I've been working on that derivation for the last two and a half days."

"My sincere apologies," she said. "But you know what they say—the math camp must go on!"

I narrowed my eyes. "Are you saying that these puzzles are more important than your campers?"

Director Verity's cheeks flushed. "No, of course not," she replied.

I aimed my chin at the cipher. "Did you put that there?" I asked.

"Well, that's not a fair question." She poked me in the ribs. "We don't want to ruin it."

Marshane rolled his eyes. "Which is a fancy way of saying no."

She opened her mouth to answer, then snapped it shut again. Marshane might have concluded that Director Verity was off the hook, but I couldn't decide which was more incriminating, that she'd tried to defend herself or that she'd just given up.

While everyone argued about the cipher's origins, I whipped out my sketchbook and dug around for a pencil, but the only writing instrument my pocket contained was a spare paintbrush. After licking the tip to loosen up the residual paint, I copied down the cipher—the last couple of letters were kind of muddled, but whatever—and tucked my faithful sketchbook back into my jeans' waistband. If the cipher could appear while we were sleeping, it could disappear while we were eating, and I strongly suspected that it was the killer's work.

The director raised her hands. "Calm down, everyone. Calm *down*." She paused for Federico to stop shaking Whistler's shoulders. "I meant to save our workshop on cryptography for later, but in light of this turn of events, it does seem appropriate to give you some kind of primer."

"What about breakfast?" Munch demanded.

"We'll eat shortly," she replied. "It will keep, won't it, Mr. Pearson?"

Mr. Pearson's lip curled up, but instead of saying no, he swallowed the lump in his throat and disappeared into the kitchen.

She set her sights on us. "Have a seat," was all she said.

I sat down next to Munch, whose scowl looked sharp enough to cut. I patted myself down, wishing that I'd thought to bring more than that one pack of Corn Nuts. The only thing I found was a lonely orange Tic Tac, but before I had a chance to offer it to Munch, he jerked a peach out of his pocket and sunk his teeth into its fuzz.

I nudged him and mouthed, *Nice.*

He half nodded, half shrugged. *You want some?* he mouthed back.

Shuddering, I shook my head. I'd sworn off eating unpeeled peaches. It felt like eating caterpillars.

"—lots of applications, from internet security to online bank transactions," Director Verity was saying. "But the substitution cipher is as fine a place to start as any."

"Bor-ing," Brooklyn said. "If I'd wanted to learn about ciphers, I would have just googled them at home."

I felt my eyes widen. She wasn't usually so snippy, at least not to the adults, but Director Verity took her attitude in stride.

"Yes, but even gifted learners must start somewhere," she replied. "And seeing as someone has kindly provided an example, I think we should soldier on."

Brooklyn made a face, but at least she held her tongue.

The director scanned the common room. "Can anyone explain the basics of a substitution cipher?"

Marshane blurted the answer: "Each letter substitutes for another letter in the alphabet, so you just have to figure out which letter substitutes for which."

"Very good," she said. I guess she didn't mind that he hadn't raised his hand. "Can anyone add anything else?" She motioned toward the kid who never spoke. "Ravi?"

"It's about looking for patterns," he said without meeting her eyes. "The most commonly used letters in the English language are *E, T,* and *A,* followed by *O, I,* and *N,* so if you figure out which letters are used most often in the cipher, you should be able to make at least a few educated guesses."

"You can look for combinations, too," Graham said. "If the same three-letter word keeps popping up, it's probably 'and' or 'the.' "

"Or 'you,' " Marshane replied.

Director Verity nodded. "There are lots of variations, but it sounds like you get the idea." She beamed at each of us in turn. "Great job, my little number crunchers!"

Ravi blushed so hard I thought his head might explode. I socked him in the shoulder by way of congratulations, then noticed Mr. Pearson brooding in the corridor. He must have reappeared during Ravi's monologue.

"Breakfast is getting cold," he said, though it sounded more like, *Your breath stinks.*

"Thank you," the director said, returning her attention to the math nerds. "Time to feed those hungry brains!"

While they scrambled to their feet, I kept an eye on Mr. Pearson. I couldn't say that he looked mad, but he didn't look glad, either. I gave him a wide berth as I trailed along behind the others, sneaking peeks in his direction when I knew he wasn't looking. The last thing I wanted to do was aggravate that man *again.*

CHAPTER 20

My sketchbook stuck to my back as I gulped down a bowl of oatmeal and trudged back into the common room for Mr. Sharp's workshop. When he handed out the paper, I took an extra for good measure, and when he turned his back, I quickly scribbled down five words: "Storage room at nine tonight."

Mr. Sharp and Ms. Gutierrez might have been seeing each other, but he was nowhere near as interesting. Whenever he had to present, he kept his eyes glued on his notes, so as soon as he started, I wadded up my secret message and lobbed it at the back of Munch's head. It bounced off his shoulder and calmly rolled under his chair, but somehow, he played it cool. When Mr. Sharp sneezed into the crook of his elbow, Munch bent down and scooped it up.

By the end of the workshop, my secret message had made

the rounds. Munch destroyed the note by tearing it into tiny pieces and devouring each one, and then we just had to wait—and not give ourselves away. Somehow, the math nerds played it cool. By 8:59, the usual suspects were assembled in the storage room. I took my normal place in the corner by the buckets, then waited for the others to quickly settle into theirs.

"I'm sure I don't need to tell you that the situation's gone from bad to critical." I pulled out my sketchbook and smacked it down on a bucket. "Now we have not one but *two* puzzles we really need to solve."

Graham shook his head. "Maybe we don't need to solve it." He scanned the room through narrowed eyes. "Maybe one of us *invented* it."

The others hemmed and hawed, but I just stood there blinking. Though it shamed me to admit it, that thought hadn't even crossed my mind.

"What about you, Munch?" he asked. When the tips of Munch's ears turned red, Graham's gaze swung across the room. "Anything to add, Marshane?"

The other boy held up his hands. "Hey, it wasn't me," he said. "And I'd take credit if it was."

That was probably true. We'd have to focus on the silent types.

"What about Ravi?" I asked. "He knows a lot about ciphers."

"So do we," Marshane replied.

"What about Whistler, then?" I pressed. "Or that kid with the glasses? What's his name?"

"Who, Keith?" Marshane replied.

"Yes, Keith!" I said elatedly. "I've barely heard him say three words. Don't they say serial killers are usually quiet and withdrawn?"

He shook his head. "It can't be him."

"How can you be so sure?" I asked.

"Because whoever came up with the cipher clearly had access to a printer."

"What are you saying?" Graham replied. "That one of the counselors is the killer?"

I scowled at no one in particular. "Or that Director Verity is."

Munch tilted his head to the side. "Why are we assuming that the killer came up with the cipher? Couldn't it have been someone else?"

That thought hadn't crossed my mind, either, but that didn't make it true. "Why would someone else invent a puzzle? Especially when the killer's already demonstrated his twisted sense of fun and games."

"This is a *math* camp," Marshane said. "We all have a twisted sense of fun and games."

I couldn't disagree with that. "All right, then, Graham, Marshane, I want you working on the cipher." They clearly knew what they were doing, and if they had a special project, it might keep them out of trouble. "The rest of us will work on figuring out the killer's clues, since we *know* who's behind them." I pulled the bobby pin out of my pocket. "And since we now have ample proof that he's got Angeline and Toby."

The bobby pin caught a shaft of sunlight and bounced it around the room, filling the math nerds' eyes with an almost eerie glow.

"I found this bobby pin, which is clearly Angeline's, under the old-fashioned typewriter producing all the clues. I also found a bunch of textbooks." I returned the trinket to my pocket, then consulted my sketchbook (since I'd scribbled down the titles as soon as I'd gotten back to my room). "*Introduction to Logic, A Concise Introduction to Logic*, and something called *The Game of Logic*—though, for the record, that one was easily the most concise."

Federico looked up from the lines he'd been tracing on his palm. "That's the Holy Trinity right there, at least when it comes to logic textbooks."

I leaned forward in my seat. "But isn't logic, you know, logical? Why would someone need to write an entire textbook on it?"

"Oh, there are all kinds of applications—law, engineering, computer science." He returned his attention to his palm. "But the *best* ones are the games."

I perked up. "The games?" That made me think of Sphinx's note.

Federico nodded. "Haven't you ever done a logic puzzle? I have to say, they're wicked fun."

"Do you think that's what this is?"

I spread the clues out on the floor. I'd been numbering them in case the order was important. Some of them were now so mangled that they looked more like confetti:

1. Satyr and Minotaur share a cabin with two other monsters.

2. Siren has a nickname.

9. Minotaur's first name begins with the same letter as Hydra's last name.

5. Phoenix wears glasses.

3. Hydra and Cyclops are involved in a not-so-secret fling.

4. Centaur, Griffin, Unicorn, and Manticore share a cabin.

6. Unicorn's nickname begins with the same letter as Manticore's first name.

8. Harpy is a girl.

7. Cyclops and Chimera share a cabin with
no other monsters.

"It could be," Federico said. He pinched the worst offender between his thumb and index finger, holding it up like a dead rat. "But it's hard to say for sure."

I pressed my lips into a line. When had it become *my* fault that the clues weren't holding up? "I have the list right here," I said as I handed him my sketchbook. "But I don't have the solution."

Federico turned the pages slowly, like the sketchbook was sacred. "Well, that's probably because you haven't used a grid," he said.

I perked up again. "A grid?" I knew something about grids.

Federico shrugged. "It's just a graphic organizer." He motioned toward the pencil tucked behind my ear. "May I?"

It was weird to see him acting so unlike his normal self—up until he'd started gushing about books and logic puzzles, I couldn't remember the last time he'd said something without bouncing—but it made me think that maybe he did know what he was doing. I handed him the pencil. If he had a problem with my earwax, he'd have to find a way to deal.

"So let's say you have three people with three different types of dogs who line them up for a race. The catch is, you have no idea which dog belongs to which person or which place the three dogs took. You only have a list of clues." He drew three three-by-three grids—one in the middle of the page, one connected on the right, and one connected on the bottom. Then he labeled the horizontal axes PEOPLE and TYPES OF DOGS and the vertical ones PLACES, and TYPES OF DOGS again. "These grids will help you work it out."

"Who are the people?" Graham replied. "And what are the types of dogs?"

Sighing, Federico scrawled BOB, BETTY, and BAR-THOLOMEW above the three columns marked PEOPLE; PIT BULL, SCHNAUZER, and GREAT DANE above the three columns labeled TYPES OF DOGS; 1ST, 2ND, and 3RD next to the three rows labeled PLACES; and PIT BULL,

| | | PEOPLE | | | TYPES OF DOGS | | |
		BOB	BETTY	BARTHOLOMEW	PIT BULL	SCHNAUZER	GREAT DANE
PLACES	1ST						
	2ND						
	3RD						
TYPES OF DOGS	PIT BULL				
	SCHNAUZER				
	GREAT DANE				

SCHNAUZER, and GREAT DANE next to the three rows labeled TYPES OF DOGS. "There, you happy now?" he asked.

Marshane shook his head. "You could have picked any type of dog, and you settled for a *schnauzer?*"

"And what kind of name is Bartholomew?" Graham asked.

Federico threw his arms up. "Those details are *not* important!" He tapped the page for emphasis. "What's important is the grids."

I picked the sketchbook up again and gave the grids a closer look. Then I flipped back a few pages and reread the killer's note.

"But this doesn't say anything about types of dogs," I said. "And we're not running a race."

"It was just a dumb example."

"But without the dogs, the race, how are we supposed to label these other two grids?" I asked.

Federico took the sketchbook back. "I really don't know," he admitted after he reread it, too. "Also, it won't work if we don't have every clue, so unless we're completely certain that we've tracked all of them down"—he snapped the sketchbook shut—"we won't be able to solve it."

"Then we'll just have to be certain." We could deal with the grid later; first, we had to find the clues. "Has anyone found any more?"

The math nerds shook their heads.

"Well, keep an eye out," I said gruffly. If the killer only won because we couldn't find his clues, I would be *very* put out.

Graham reviewed the note that I'd gotten from the killer. "If this *is* a logic puzzle, we're gonna have to figure out which monster is which person. Then we'll know who the killer is."

"And who he's gonna kill," Marshane said grimly.

"He's not gonna get the chance. We *will* find Angeline and Toby before the killer can off them." I snatched the note away from Graham. "At least we already have one piece of the puzzle figured out."

Federico shook his head. "The story makes it sound like there's only one victim. And if this *is* a logic puzzle, then there's only one solution."

I tilted my head to the side. "Maybe it didn't mention them because the killer knew that they'd already be out of commission." I locked eyes with the others. "Which, unfortunately, means he's coming after someone else."

CHAPTER 21

We spent the rest of the night trying to figure out the grids (or just skip straight to the solution), but we didn't make much progress. By the time we had to go to bed, we'd only managed to come up with a list of scribbled-out guesses.

I dismissed the other math nerds, then tripped upstairs to my room. Moonlight spilled through the sliding door, bathing Angeline's cold bed in a ghostly, washed-out glow. I shook off the creeps that tried to shiver down my spine. She *wasn't* dead. She couldn't be.

Brooklyn looked up from the suitcase she'd never bothered to unpack. "Have a meltdown if you must, but keep your bodily fluids to yourself."

I was too tired to fight back. "Why do you do that?" I asked.

"Why do I do *what*?" she growled.

"Treat everyone like sludge," I said.

Brooklyn rolled her eyes as she flopped onto her bunk. "I don't treat *everyone* like sludge, just useless hacks like you."

I didn't take her bait, just stood there blinking, thinking. She pretended to ignore me, but I could tell I'd gotten to her.

"Do you want to talk about it?"

"With you?" she asked, scoffing.

My only answer was to nod.

Brooklyn scratched her nose and sighed. "My dad is in the Air Force, all right? He's been on, like, six tours of duty, so now he seems, I don't know, different."

Though I'd hoped she would open up, I hadn't expected her to. "Is he angry?" I whispered. I'd certainly be angry if I'd been forced to go to war.

"Sometimes," she admitted. "But most of the time, he just seems . . . empty. Like he left the most important pieces of himself back there." She dragged a hand across her face. "Still, that's no excuse. I've been a moron, and I'm sorry."

"Apology accepted," I replied. "That must have taken lots of guts."

Brooklyn rolled her eyes. "Now you sound like my therapist."

I grinned despite myself. "You know what they say about great minds."

"Don't think this little chat makes us besties now," she said.

I tilted my head to the side. "Do you think we could be friends?"

She made an unflattering noise that sounded exactly like a snort, but just before she rolled away, I spied her mouth. And it was smiling.

I couldn't help but smile, too, as I changed into my pajamas and burrowed deep under the covers. It was way colder in these mountains than I'd ever thought it could be (or maybe that was just because my spirits were chilled to the bone). Either way, I couldn't sleep, so I clicked my flashlight on and cracked my dog-eared sketchbook open. But the clues were no more understandable than they'd been earlier. I dug my fists into my eyes, but the darn words just kept swimming. Maybe Brooklyn had it right. Maybe I *was* a useless hack.

I pushed those thoughts out of my head. Moping wouldn't solve this problem *or* save Angeline and Toby. After drawing a deep breath, I turned over the last page and dug out a pencil stub. I needed to get out of my head, let my thoughts float for a while. The only way I knew how to do that was by sketching, sketching, sketching.

I started with some random doodles. Doodling usually calmed me down, but tonight, it revved me up. I turned the page over again and pulled my phone out of my pocket. If I wanted to calm down, I would have to go all in.

I couldn't help but grin as I thumbed through the pictures I'd taken. There was Munch. There was Marshane. The one of Toby in that apron nearly made me laugh out loud. But then I remembered he was missing, and the laugh died in my throat. Toby was the kindest, gentlest man I'd ever met. He shouldn't have been made to suffer for my sheer stupidity.

Blinking the tears out of my eyes, I laid a grid over his face. My fingers knew what to do next, so my brain had time to wander as I penciled in the lines. Before long, the list of clues was steadily cycling through my brain along with our scribbled-out guesses. If Minotaur shared a cabin with three other monsters, it had to be one of the boys. And if Harpy was a girl, it *couldn't* be one of the boys.

By the time I realized I'd labeled the horizontal axis MONSTERS and the vertical one PEOPLE and was penciling in our names, I couldn't blink, could barely breathe. *This* was the piece that we'd been missing. *This* was the start of the solution.

We didn't need an L-shaped grid. We needed one enormous one.

I couldn't wait to show my work to the others the next morning. I threw on my nearest clothes, then stuffed my sketchbook down my shirt and hightailed it out of there. When I slapped my sketchbook down and Federico's eyes lit up, I knew that I was onto something.

But the grid was useless on its own; we still had to fill it in. And before we could do *that*, we had to finish labeling it. We put the monsters on one side, but the people wouldn't fit. Even after we added ourselves, the other math nerds (Oliver, Whistler, Ravi, Keith, and Brooklyn), the counselors (Mr. Pearson, Mr. Sharp, and Ms. Gutierrez), and Director Verity, we were still one person short.

We spent the rest of the day trying to figure out who it should be.

"It should be Angeline," Graham said. "She's been a part of the camp from the very beginning."

We were back down at the amphitheater, soaking up some much-needed sun while the director tried to teach us about animals' survival and competing population-growth rates. We were supposed to be working on our graphs (trout versus mayfly), but every time she turned her back, I would flip my paper over and tinker with the grid. I'd drawn it so many times I could have drawn it in my sleep.

"We can't add Angeline without adding Toby, too," I growled. "He also disappeared, you know."

"Yes, but your stepdad wasn't supposed to be here," Graham replied.

I threw my arms up. "Yeah, well, neither was I!"

I must have screamed that last line, because Director Verity stopped and glanced over her shoulder. "Are you quite all right, Esther?"

"I'm fine," I said through gritted teeth. "I must have gotten a Corn Nut stuck in my throat."

"Well, be careful," she replied. "I'm afraid emergency services take some time to get up here."

Was that supposed to be some kind of threat?

Stretching to cover my shiver, I returned my attention to the grid. I straddled my bench so I could look at the grid from a new perspective, but I only succeeded in scratching my legs on the log's gnarly bark. When a speckled beetle scurried across my paper, I didn't flick it away. It could probably solve this puzzle as easily as I could.

Marshane lay down on his log. As he was so fond of telling us, he thought of himself as the think tank, not the scribe. "Didn't we decide to leave out Angeline and Toby?"

Graham rolled his eyes. "Then who gets the last slot?"

I sat up straight. "Archimedes. Has to be."

I didn't know why I hadn't thought of it before. I already suspected him, but he couldn't be Sphinx if we didn't include him. With a quaking hand, I quickly added his name.

The grid was ready to go.

I started penciling in some of the clues I remembered, but before I had a chance to get into a groove, Director Verity said it was time to head back.

While we were picking up our stuff, Marshane sidled up to me. "We did it," he whispered.

"You did *what*?" I whispered back.

"We decrypted the cipher!" Graham replied, appearing on my other side.

I looked back and forth between them, searching for some sign of deception, but the smiles on their faces were too open to be fake.

Graham held out a scrap of paper that had been folded in half. "It says, 'If you know what's good for you, then you'll stay out of my workroom.'"

I crinkled my nose. Whatever I'd thought it would say, that definitely wasn't it.

Graham unfolded the scrap, revealing the contents of the cipher in his surprisingly sleek handwriting:

BO YKU DJKW WAFT'S RKKI OKQ YKU, TAMJ YKU'GG STFY KUT
KO HY WKQDQKKH
IF YOU KNOW WHAT'S GOOD FOR YOU, THEN YOU'LL STAY OUT
OF MY WORKROOM

"At first, we thought the *K* had to be an *E*," he said.

"Or an *A*," Marshane replied.

"But then Marshane pointed out that *Y-K-U* appeared three times, once as a contraction, so it seemed a lot more likely that the *K* was another vowel, *O*, and that *Y-K-U* was 'you.'"

"Once we had that *K* was *O*, we plugged that into the cipher and saw what else we could come up with. When

K-U-T turned into *O-U-T*, 'out,' we knew we had to be dealing with a classic keyword cipher."

I snatched the scrap out of his hands. "That isn't much of a cipher."

Marshane snatched it out of mine. "That's because of the keyword. So let's say it was 'Esther'—or *E-S-T-H-R*, since you can't use a letter twice." He scribbled that down on the scrap. "Then you start at the beginning of the alphabet, so your *A*s would become *E*s, your *B*s would become *S*s, your *C*s would become *T*s, your *D*s would become *H*s, and your *E*s would become *R*s."

A B C D E
E S T H R

While Marshane quickly wrote down the rest of the alphabet, Graham picked up the explanation: "Then you keep going with the letters that don't appear in the keyword— starting with the *A*, of course—so in Marshane's made-up example, the *F* would become an *A*, the *G* would become a *B*, the *H* would become a *C*, and the *I* would become a *D*."

A B C D E F G H I
E S T H R A B C D

"But then you'd have to skip *E* since it appeared in the keyword, so your *J* would become *F*."

Graham nodded absently. "You would keep going like that until you got to the *T* in the normal alphabet—"

"Which would become *Q*," Marshane added.

"—and then the rest of the letters would just be themselves," Graham said as if Marshane hadn't cut in. "Since *T* is the last letter alphabetically in 'Esther,' the letters after it don't shift."

"So if we go back to *our* cipher"—Marshane flipped the scrap back over—"as soon as we knew the *T* was *T*, we also knew the letters after it had to be just themselves, too."

"Then we figured out the rest pretty easily," Graham said.

It felt like my brain was about to set itself on fire. I might have been a math nerd now, but their explanation just confirmed that they were on a different level. Not because Graham and Marshane were any smarter than I was, but because they'd put in the time to actually learn all this stuff.

"The only thing I want to know is what the message really *means*." I waited for lightning to strike, and just like that, it did. "The workroom must be the shed."

Graham exchanged a loaded look with Marshane. "It *could* be the shed," he said.

"Unless it's the storage room."

I almost laughed in Marshane's face. The workroom *had* to be the shed; that was the only explanation. But then the director glanced at us over her shoulder. She was halfway up the path that eventually led back to the lodge, so I grabbed the scrap of paper, crumpled it into a ball, and shoved it into my pocket. There was still a decent chance she was our mass murderer.

While Graham raced to catch up, I purposely hung back. I needed time to digest and space to let my brain wander, so I plodded along, mostly staring at nothing, until I realized that I was staring at something—and that that something was pink.

Then the something moved.

I blinked despite myself. There weren't very many pink things in the natural world. A flower could have been pink, but it definitely couldn't have moved. Before I could decide whether or not to chase the something, my feet were flying toward the woods.

Director Verity whirled around. "Esther, where are you going?"

I didn't bother to reply, just plunged into the restless trees. If I'd really just seen what I thought I'd just seen, there was no time to lose. Angeline must have escaped, but she was lost or confused. A few days in the company of a mass murderer, and anyone would go crazy. It was my job to save her.

Voices called after me, but I paid them no heed. If I stopped to explain, I might lose Angeline. I didn't stop running until I was well out of sight, at which point I let myself pause to survey my surroundings (and swallow mouthfuls of air). The something was gone, but I'd kept my eyes on the spot. As long as I kept heading in that general direction, I'd find it eventually.

I only had to cover ten yards before I saw it again through a gap in the bushes. I veered instinctively toward the something but also toward the footsteps that were hot on my heels. If Angeline stayed on this line, I might not catch up to her before they caught up to me.

A boulder appeared in my path, but when I swerved to avoid it, I ended up smacking into a sapling instead. I bounced off the bendy trunk and hit the ground, hard, but I didn't cry out, just lurched back to my feet. If Angeline didn't slow down, I'd never be able to save her.

I was about to give up when I spotted the something again—and this time, it didn't move. Putting on a fresh burst of speed, I half hobbled, half sprinted toward that violent pink smudge. Branches scratched my cheeks and whipped into my eyes, but I just plowed ahead. It had definitely stopped.

Just before I reached the something, I stumbled across a ravine, so I scrambled down one side, then scurried up the other. At the top of the next ridge, I finally laid eyes on it. But it wasn't Angeline. It was a twisted-up sweater.

I approached it warily, like it might rip my throat out at any second. But the sweater was just a sweater (though it was kind of dirty). I poked it with a stick, then tentatively picked it up. It had gotten tangled on a broken-off branch, so I had to unwind it. When it started unraveling, I winced despite myself.

As far as sweaters went, it was a doozy. It looked more like a jacket than a sweater, but instead of a zipper, it had a row of bright pink buttons and a frothy lace edge. I'd never seen Angeline in this particular sweater, but it *was* her signature color. As I brushed off the dirt, I noticed the jagged tear in the sleeve.

It was covered with blood.

CHAPTER 22

I was still gaping at the tear when some of the other math nerds reached me. Graham was the first one on the scene, but Marshane was hot on his heels. They took one look at the sweater and stumbled back a step.

"Whoa," was all Graham said.

"Where did you find that?" Marshane asked.

I motioned toward the broken branch. "It was hanging over there."

Marshane looked around. "Where did it come from?" he replied.

I scowled. "Where do you think?"

He opened his mouth to answer, then snapped it shut again. We were still just standing there gaping when several more math nerds caught up. Munch planted both hands on his knees, and Federico emptied the contents of his stomach on an anthill.

He wiped his mouth off. "Is it Angel—?"

I cut him off with a stern look. Director Verity had arrived.

"What's going on here?" she demanded, looking back and forth between us. She'd been smart enough to wear a pair of flats, but she was still going to have to junk them. Also, her hair was coming out of its neat bun.

I was tempted to hide the sweater, but that would only make things worse. "I'm sorry, Director Verity." I lowered my gaze. "I just thought I saw . . . someone."

"Who would you expect to see out here?" Then she noticed the sweater. "Oh."

What kind of an answer was *that*? Maybe I'd been too cryptic. After drawing a deep breath, I held up the bloodied sweater. "I think it's Angeline's."

Director Verity paled, but before I could press her for details, she stuck out her chin. "How could it be Angeline's?" she asked. "You know as well as I do that Angeline *went home*."

I opened my mouth to answer, then swiftly snapped it shut again. If she wanted to play dumb, I would just have to play dumber.

Director Verity held out her hand. "Give it to me."

I licked my lips. If I gave it to her, I'd be sacrificing my best piece of evidence.

Director Verity trembled. "I said, give it to me."

I snuck a peek at Graham, who nodded (barely). But when I glanced at Marshane, he just shook his head.

"Esther," she said grimly, "I won't ask you again." When I still hesitated, she pressed her lips into a line. "Please don't make me call Mr. Renfro."

She couldn't have hit me harder if she'd punched me in the stomach. There was only one reason to drag Toby into this hot mess, and that was to threaten him. Reluctantly, I gave her the sweater.

She wadded it into a ball and tucked it under her arm. It all but disappeared into the folds of her blue blazer. "Now, I suggest that you get back on the trail." She surveyed the math nerds. "*All* of you."

I wanted to stand up, stand out, but I couldn't take risks with Toby's life. When I leaped across the ravine and slowly trudged back to the path, the math nerds followed tiredly.

When we emerged from the dense woods, we found the others waiting for us, some patiently, some less patiently. Ravi and Oliver wouldn't look me in the eyes—Oliver must have told Ravi that I was a psycho—and Whistler was too busy whistling the *Guardians of the Galaxy* soundtrack to notice our return. Sighing, I shuffled past Munch—and felt another scrap of paper slide magically into my palm. As soon as Director Verity assumed her place up at the front, I unfolded it:

Griffin and Harpy haven't been to the top of Lookout Hill.

While I'd been chasing ghosts, the killer had planted another clue.

By the time I got back to my room, I was determined to solve the puzzle. I slipped off my shoes and folded myself into my bunk, tucking my legs up around me. I hadn't been able to sit cross-legged since I'd hit my last growth spurt, but it was the thought that counted.

I'd opened my sketchbook so many times in the past few days that I could find the right page by feel as much as by sight, so instead of focusing on the pages, I focused on the grid. I'd just added Archimedes's name when the door crashed into the wall, admitting a blast of stagnant air. The pages of my sketchbook shuddered as Brooklyn stomped into the room and let the door bang shut behind her. I didn't try to say anything, but when she cracked the sliding door, admitting a blast of fresh air, I blurted, "*What* are you doing?"

"Friends don't let friends stink," she said, "or go traipsing through the woods."

Somehow, I knew this was her way of trying to start a conversation. "I thought I saw someone," I said.

She shifted her weight onto one foot and stuck both hands

on her hips. "When are you going to accept that Angeline went home?" she asked.

I motioned toward the closet. "When her stuff Disapparates?"

Brooklyn stalked across the room and pulled the door open with a jerk. Except for a pair of lonely hangers, the closet was completely empty.

I scrambled to my feet. "Angeline's duffel was right there!"

"Admit it, Esther," she replied. "You've lost touch with reality."

I crossed the room in three great strides and checked the closet for myself, but Angeline's duffel was gone. It was well and truly gone (though I could still see its outline in the fine layer of dust).

I slid slowly down the wall, landing on the floorboards with a *thud*. I wasn't going crazy. Angeline had been kidnapped, and Toby had been kidnapped, too. The killer had left their stuff behind to lure me into his trap. He must have come back and retrieved Angeline's duffel to keep messing with my head.

Brooklyn sat down next to me. "I know what's going on," she said.

I swallowed, hard. "You do?"

She nodded solemnly. "Frankly, I'm appalled that the counselors haven't picked up on your little murder mystery."

I dragged a hand under my nose. "Why haven't you enlightened them?"

"Because I knew you'd self-destruct." She fiddled with her ponytail. "But maybe now I want to help."

"Then you admit that there's a killer?"

"I admit that *you* think there's a killer."

"There *is* a killer," I replied.

"Then prove it," Brooklyn said.

I felt myself deflate. She must have known I couldn't prove it, not without that bloody sweater. Not without the puzzle solved.

Brooklyn huffed. "What do you need?"

"To prove the killer's real?" I asked.

"No, to prove fairies exist." When I just gawked at her, she hissed, "Yes, of *course* that's what I meant!"

I lowered my gaze. "I don't know," I admitted, sighing. "Maybe I'm not smart enough."

She pushed herself back to her feet. "If you're just going to sulk, then I'm going to go to the bathroom." And with that, she disappeared.

After the door swung closed behind her, I crawled back over to my bunk. My sketchbook was still just sitting there, practically daring me to fail. There was a good chance that I would. That I'd fail dramatically. That I'd let Angeline and Toby down.

But they needed me to try.

After doodling some wolves to give myself time to calm down, I decided to just start from scratch. With a fresh pair of eyes, I considered each and every clue:

1. Satyr and Minotaur share a cabin with two other monsters.
2. Siren has a nickname.
3. Hydra and Cyclops are involved in a not-so-secret fling.
4. Centaur, Griffin, Unicorn, and Manticore share a cabin.
5. Phoenix wears glasses.
6. Unicorn's nickname begins with the same letter as Manticore's first name.
7. Cyclops and Chimera share a cabin with no other monsters.
8. Harpy is a girl.
9. Minotaur's first name begins with the same letter as Hydra's last name.
10. Griffin and Harpy haven't been to the top of Lookout Hill.

There was nothing to do but jump in with both feet and do it. Since the first clue made it clear that cabin assignments were important, I rearranged my list, starting with Ms. Gutierrez and Director Verity, then Mr. Sharp and

Mr. Pearson, then the boys in Cabin Gamma (Munch, Marshane, Ravi, and Oliver), then the boys in Cabin Delta (Graham, Keith, Whistler, and Federico), then Brooklyn and me. Then, finally, Archimedes.

	SPHINX	CENTAUR	UNICORN	GRIFFIN	PEGASUS	MANTICORE	MINOTAUR	HARPY	SIREN	HYDRA	CYCLOPS	PHOENIX	GORGON	CHIMERA	SATYR
MS. GUTIERREZ															
DIRECTOR VERITY															
MR. SHARP															
MR. PEARSON															
MUNCH															
MARSHANE															
RAVI															
OLIVER															
GRAHAM															
KEITH															
WHISTLER															
FEDERICO															
BROOKLYN															
ME															
ARCHIMEDES															

After drawing a deep breath, I returned my attention to the clues. If Satyr and Minotaur shared a cabin with two other monsters, then they had to be math nerds (and not Brooklyn or me). I exed out the extra boxes in both columns, then set my sights on the next clue. If Siren had a nickname, it was clearly Munch or Whistler. I exed out the extra boxes in Siren's column, too.

Clue number three was also helpful. If Hydra and Cyclops were involved in a not-so-secret fling, then they had to be Mr. Sharp and Ms. Gutierrez. I exed out the other boxes in both columns *and* the other boxes in both rows, then moved on to the next clue.

It was a lot like the first. If Centaur, Griffin, Unicorn, and Manticore shared a cabin, then they had to be the math nerds in Cabin Gamma or Cabin Delta. As I exed out the extra boxes in each of those four columns, I couldn't help but feel like I was making decent progress. And the fifth clue kept it coming. If Phoenix wore glasses, that instantly narrowed it down to Keith or Mr. Sharp. But since I already knew that Mr. Sharp *couldn't* be Phoenix, that meant I also knew that Phoenix had to be Keith.

I exed out the other boxes in Keith's row *and* Phoenix's column. Then I tackled the sixth clue. It was more complicated than the others I'd encountered, but I didn't let that faze me, just calmed down and took it slow. The first two words implied that Unicorn had a nickname, which meant that, like Siren, it had to be Munch or Whistler. I reread the second half, then reviewed the other exes I'd stuck in Manticore's column. Since I'd already decided that Manticore was one of the math nerds in Cabin Gamma or Cabin Delta, I just had to figure out which math nerds had names that began with *M* or *W*. As it turned out, Marshane was the only math nerd whose name fit, which meant that he was Manticore. Which meant that Munch was Unicorn.

My pulse throbbed in my ears as I exed out the other boxes. I looked back over the grid to give myself time to calm down and noticed that the only empty box anywhere in Siren's column was the one that belonged to Whistler. I stuck exes in the rest of the boxes in his row, then looked back over it again. But as far as I could tell, there were no more easy gets, so I went on to the next clue.

If Cyclops and Chimera shared a cabin with no other monsters, then that narrowed it down to Brooklyn, Director Verity, one of the counselors, or me. I stuck exes in the extra boxes in Chimera's column, but Cyclops's extra boxes were already exed out. Clue number eight was even kinder: if Harpy was a girl, then the only options left were Brooklyn, Director Verity, or, once again, me.

I exed out the extra boxes, then moved on the ninth clue. It was another doozy, but luckily, I already knew quite a few bits of information about Hydra *and* Minotaur. Since I'd narrowed Hydra down to Mr. Sharp or Ms. Gutierrez, I just had to figure out which math nerds had names that began with *S* or *G*. Once again, there was only one, which meant that Minotaur was Graham and Hydra was Ms. Gutierrez.

I couldn't help but grin as I exed out the other boxes and drew a fortifying breath. But when I surveyed my work, the smile melted off my face. I was still making decent progress, but I was down to the last clue.

The hairs on the back of my neck prickled as I set my sights on the tenth clue. I'd gotten the impression that I was being watched, and this clue confirmed my hunch. Somehow, the killer knew who'd been to the top of Lookout Hill and who'd stayed back down at the lodge. But in the end, it didn't matter. If I wanted to get Angeline and Toby back, I had no choice but to keep going.

I looked back over my work. At this point, it was safe to say my only options for Griffin were Ravi, Oliver, or Federico. But Federico had been with us when we broke into the shed, so I knew he'd been to the top. I also knew that Ravi hadn't—he never, ever broke the rules, and Director Verity had made it clear that the hill and the cabin were off-limits—and the same went for Oliver. But then I remembered I'd made Oliver come with us on our first ill-fated trip, which made Ravi Griffin.

Harpy was even easier. *I'd* been to the top of Lookout Hill, and Director Verity had, too (when she came to collect us). Which made Brooklyn Harpy.

But now I was out of clues. I felt my shoulders droop as I gnawed on the end of my pencil. I was clearly missing something, but what exactly was I missing? Another clue? A bigger brain? I skipped back up to the top and slowly worked my way back down. And I did work a few more out.

If Satyr and Minotaur shared a cabin—and if Minotaur was Graham—then Satyr couldn't be Oliver, which meant that it was Federico. And when I exed out the rest of the boxes in his row, I found that the only box left in Centaur's column was Oliver's.

Sadly, that still left Sphinx and Pegasus (and Gorgon and Chimera). I scanned the list for clues about any of these monsters and found one about Chimera. If it and Cyclops shared a cabin—and if Cyclops was Mr. Sharp—then it had to be Mr. Pearson.

But none of the clues mentioned Sphinx, Gorgon, *or* Pegasus.

How could I solve the logic puzzle without clues about those monsters? I knew *I* wasn't Sphinx, but even if I factored that in, I couldn't eliminate Archimedes or Director Verity.

In other words, I'd failed.

I snapped my pencil in half, shoved my sketchbook off my lap, and flopped back onto my bunk. The mattress sagged beneath my weight, but the pillow crinkled eagerly. Like someone had replaced the filling with tiny pieces of paper.

I reached into the pillowcase and withdrew a scrap of paper. My fingers recognized the texture even as my eyes took in the words:

```
Pegasus has sneaked out of its cabin after
dark.
```

Before I had a chance to process what the words might mean, the door to Cabin Epsilon creaked open. I leaped to my feet, ready to defend myself if necessary, but it was only Brooklyn. Her eyes were as wide as two pools of spilled brown paint—and her fingers were curled around a soggy scrap of paper.

I snatched the clue out of her hands. "Where did you find this?" I demanded.

"In the bathroom," she replied. "It looked like it had been there for at least a day or two."

I drew a bracing breath. This could be the one that would sort everything out, that would make everything clear. Was I ready, *really* ready? Once I knew the truth, there would be no going back.

"Well?" Brooklyn demanded. "Are you going to open it or what?"

Slowly, I uncurled the clue:

```
Gorgon and Hydra share a cabin with no
other monsters.
```

I'd spent so much time wrestling with the logic puzzle that I knew at once what this clue meant. Hydra was Ms. Gutierrez, so Director Verity was Gorgon.

Which made me Pegasus.

Which made Archimedes Sphinx.

Brooklyn leaned over my shoulder. "What does it mean? What does it *mean*?"

I opened my mouth to answer, but no sound managed to come out. I probably should have seen this coming. I *was* the causer of problems. But I was also the solver, so it made a crooked kind of sense. If anyone was going to give Archimedes our solution, it was going to be me.

"It means I'm gonna die," I said.

CHAPTER 23

I clutched my sketchbook to my chest as I ascended Lookout Hill less than twenty minutes later, feeling naked and exposed in the middle of the road. The packed dirt amplified my footsteps, broadcasting my location to anyone in the general vicinity, but then, I no longer had a good reason to hide. If Archimedes hadn't guessed that I was coming, he would figure it out soon enough.

Math nerds fanned out behind me like a peacock's open tail, Munch and Marshane on one side, Graham and Federico on the other. They'd insisted on coming—to guarantee my safety or something ludicrous like that.

But this was a job for only one.

"Wait here," I told them, gesturing toward a nearby bush. "I don't see a reason to risk *all* of our lives."

"And I don't see a reason to risk *your* life," Graham said. "Let's just call the police."

"We'd never convince Director Verity to let us borrow her satellite phone. Even if she isn't Sphinx, she still thinks Angeline's grandpa came to pick her up." I sent the cabin a sideways glance. "If there's even a chance they're still alive, we have to take it while we have it. The police would have to get search warrants, and we can't wait that long."

Graham's jaw trembled, but at least he held his tongue.

"I could come with you," Munch blurted, then lowered his gaze. "If you want me to."

For a second, I wavered. I'd already endangered Munch's life more times than I cared to admit, so what was the problem with one more? It would have been nice to have a second, especially if I had to fight to get Angeline and Toby out. But if there was even a chance that they were already dead, I couldn't endanger Munch's life again. The only math nerd who'd be putting her life on the line was me.

I patted his shoulder. "I know you've got my back, but I can't risk your neck again."

Munch rolled his eyes. "That's the dumbest thing I've ever heard."

"Hey, I got that off a postcard! A specialized team of one-line writers slaved over that sentence for days."

Munch's toothy grin slowly melted into a frown. "Just don't die, okay?"

Marshane waved that off. "But if you *do* die, can I have your sketchbook?"

I half laughed, half sobbed. I would have slugged him again, but Federico beat me to it. Marshane made a show of massaging his shoulder.

I couldn't help but gulp. I would have traded my best paintbrush for another five minutes with these clowns, but that was exactly why I couldn't wait. "Well, I guess this is it."

Munch offered me his last Swiss Roll. "It's not much of a last meal, but it's the best that I can do."

"Oh, no, that's all right," I said. "You'll taste it much more than I will." I forced myself to smile. "See you on the other side."

I really hoped that wouldn't turn out to be some kind of premonition.

The narrow road cut through the grass with the precision of a lawnmower, so nothing tickled my cheeks or tugged at my ankles. Still, my feet felt heavy as I made my way up to the porch. When a pine-scented breeze suddenly swept through the clearing, I actually stopped and spread my arms out. I hadn't thought that I could sweat everywhere that I was sweating.

The porch groaned under my feet as I climbed the sloping steps and cautiously rang the bell, and I had a fleeting image of the floorboards giving out and dumping me into a pit. There was probably a dungeon down there, which meant that I was on the verge of meeting a real, live skeleton (or maybe just a real, *dead* skeleton). But then the image faded, and shuffling footsteps approached. As the front door creaked open, I couldn't help but brace myself.

I'd never really wondered what Archimedes looked like, but even if I had, I wouldn't have come close to the truth. He looked more like a cowboy than a former professor, with faded jeans, a long-sleeved shirt, and a shiny belt buckle that easily could have doubled as a dinner plate. He was slightly hunched over, and his hair was as silver as his belt buckle, but I didn't let looks deceive me. He was a killer, no doubt about it.

He just stood there breathing, and I just stood there waiting. If my whole life was flashing before my eyes, I was missing it somehow.

When I decided I'd rather die than keep waiting and wondering, I cleared my throat. "Archimedes?" I asked softly.

He cocked his head to the side. "I've answered to that name before."

I shifted uncertainly. I hadn't thought past introductions. I must have assumed he'd murder me, and yet here we were, staring back and forth at each other. Finally, I locked my knees and stated the obvious: "I solved Sphinx's puzzle."

If I'd had any doubts, they would have blown away like

smoke as soon as those words had left my mouth. He didn't try to pretend he didn't know what I was talking about, just waved me into the house and retreated toward the back.

I took the hint and eased myself over the threshold. As soon as I stepped inside, the door started to close. I resisted the urge to run away screaming or, worse, glance behind me. No matter what else I did, I wouldn't give the boys away.

Though Archimedes had faded to a barely visible smudge, I took a few extra seconds to survey my surroundings. The living room was just a living room with a lumpy plaid couch, and though there *was* a shotgun, it was mounted over the fireplace. An old, beat-up umbrella stand was guarding the window, so maybe that explained the shotgun Munch and Oliver had seen. There was no coffee table, just several stacks of old textbooks that had been pushed up next to each other to create a (mostly) level surface. I craned my neck to read the spines, but the lighting was too poor.

By the time I remembered to look for Archimedes, he'd disappeared. I crept after him, my muscles ready for action. Behind the living room was a kitchen that didn't appear to get much use, and next to the kitchen was a dining room that seemed to get too much. The table was piled high with notebooks, three-ring binders, and what looked like the blueprints for our very own lodge.

Though I could hear Archimedes, it took me a moment to spot him. He was rooting around in a cupboard next to the refrigerator. Unfortunately, his belt buckle kept getting in the way.

"I know Charlotte keeps you kids practically stuffed to the gills"—he finally resurfaced with two cans of sliced peaches—"but I'm afraid we're on prison rations around here."

I tried to ignore his use of the word "prison." "Who's Charlotte?" I asked.

"Oh, that's right," he replied as he set the cans down on the counter. "I forgot she makes you kids call her Director Verity."

"So you know her," I said slowly. She'd already mentioned that he did, but it seemed like a good idea to keep him talking.

"Know her?" he replied as he produced a grimy can opener. "Why, I taught Charlotte Verity everything she knows." He cranked open both cans, then raised one to his lips and expertly slurped out a peach. After wiping off his mouth, he offered me the other can. "I trust that you like peaches?"

I still wasn't hungry, but I didn't want to upset him. "Who doesn't like peaches?" I asked. Munch must have been rubbing off on me.

Archimedes didn't answer, just slid the can across the counter. I caught it at the last second, slopping a spoonful of peach juice over the side of the can. He didn't seem to care.

"They're only store-bought," he went on as he took another slurp. After wiping off his mouth again, he smiled, revealing a row of crooked teeth. "I've been running low on supplies."

There was the leer I'd been waiting for. We must have been getting closer to the murdering part. If I wanted to keep breathing, I needed him to keep talking.

"Do you only eat canned food?" I asked.

He nodded. "Except for Vienna sausage. I don't eat those slimy little turds. Clearly, the Viennese have never had bratwurst before."

I nearly choked on a bite of peach. If this dude hadn't kidnapped and possibly killed Toby, we might have been best friends.

Archimedes set his can down. "Well, then, let's have a look."

"A look at *what*?" I asked. Did he want to inspect my teeth before he actually killed me?

He motioned toward my sketchbook. "Didn't you say that you'd solved it?"

"Oh, right," I said, blushing. It was like I'd forgotten why I'd come in the first place. I found a relatively clean spot on the counter to lean my sketchbook against, then fumbled through the pages. But my hands were shaking so badly that I couldn't get a decent grip.

Archimedes squinted at me. "What's the matter, kid? You're not gonna faint, are you?"

I opened my mouth to answer, but no sound came out.

He massaged the back of his neck. "Please don't tell me you lied. I would have shared my peaches even if you hadn't solved it."

"No, that's not it," I replied, grabbing hold of the counter to steady myself. "I guess I'm just wondering what will happen next. Are you gonna kill me straight out, or will you torture me first? And if I say, 'No, don't kill me, I've got a lot to live for,' will that make any difference?"

Archimedes shook his head. "Let's take this one step at a time." He motioned toward the chair behind me. "Why don't you have a seat?"

I couldn't tell if this was an order or a casual suggestion, but I sat down, anyway. When my hands started to shake, I squeezed my sketchbook tighter. I might have been dueling with the devil, but I wasn't about to let him see my fear.

"I guess we should start with the easy ones," I said as I flipped open my sketchbook. "Graham is Minotaur, Marshane is Manticore, and Ravi is Griffin. Also, Mr. Sharp and Mr. Pearson are Cyclops and Chimera, and Ms. Gutierrez and Director Verity are Hydra and Gorgon. I know these answers don't match up with every detail from your note—the last time I checked, Ravi's head was definitely *not* stuck in the clouds—but maybe you wanted to force me to use each and every clue?"

He half nodded, half shrugged.

I decided to keep going. "That leaves Federico as Satyr, Whistler as Siren, Oliver as Centaur, Keith as Phoenix, Munch as Unicorn, and Brooklyn as Harpy. That makes me"—I gulped—"Pegasus." Then I set my sketchbook down and looked him straight in the eyes. If I was about to meet my doom, I wanted to see it coming. "And that makes you Sphinx."

I tensed myself for his attack, but he just finished off his peaches and let out a healthy burp.

"Fifty percent," was all he said.

"What do you mean, 'fifty percent'?"

"Out of Sphinx and Pegasus," he said. "I don't remember who the other monsters were, but they weren't important, anyway. Now, that might be an F when you're twelve or thirteen, but it's a solid C at the postsecondary level." He added his empty can to the heap of trash in the corner. "Excellent job."

"Wait a second," I replied, planting both hands on the table. "Are you saying I got it *wrong*?"

"On the contrary," he said, "I'm saying you got it right. Most of it, anyway."

Hope leaped in my chest. "So I'm not Pegasus?" I asked.

"Oh, no, you're Pegasus," he said as he whipped out a pocket knife, a sleek-looking black thing. I braced myself again for his attack, but instead of unsheathing the blade, he used one of the attachments to dig the gunk out from under his nails. "I'm just not Sphinx."

My eyes bulged. "You're not?"

"No," a familiar voice said, "*I* am."

CHAPTER 24

I whirled around, knocking the blueprints off the table. They floated to the floor as Angeline emerged out of the shadows. Her hands were on her hips, and she was grinning gleefully.

"I knew you'd do it!" she said. "I knew it would be you!"

I leaped out of my seat. "What are you doing here?" I asked. "I thought you were freaking dead."

She'd been coming toward me with outstretched arms, but this announcement made her stop. "Why did you think I was dead?"

"Because you vanished," I replied. "I got that creepy note, and then you were nowhere to be found."

Angeline blinked. "Well, I had to disappear," she said. "How could I have planted clues if I'd been tied down by workshops?"

"Then why didn't you take your stuff—and why did you

come back to get it?" I backed up against the wall. I'd never believed in ghosts, but then, I'd never believed in math camps, either. "Angeline, I thought you were *dead*."

She frowned. "I wanted you to take it seriously, but maybe not *that* seriously . . ."

Archimedes cleared his throat.

"What do you think?" she asked, flinching.

He aimed his can opener at her. "I think it's time to come clean."

She flopped down into the chair that I'd just launched myself out of. "Oh, all right," she said.

I didn't sit back down, just eyed Angeline warily. If she really was Sphinx, then was *she* going to kill me? I could probably take her in a fair fight, but Archimedes was a wild card. That belt buckle looked like it could do some serious damage.

I was about to cut my losses and just make a break for it when I remembered Toby. Angeline might have turned up (and as the killer, no less), but he could still be out there somewhere, rotting in her secret lair. I didn't have a chance to ask her if she knew where Toby was before she launched into a monologue.

"Everything started," she said grandly, "with Mom's First Stupid Problem. Only a few kids even try it, but Mom keeps putting it out there."

At least that caught my attention. "Wait a second," I replied. "Director Verity is your *mom*?"

Angeline nodded. "And Archimedes is my grandpa, but that's beside the point."

The wheels in my head started churning. "So she wasn't lying," I mumbled. Angeline *had* gone home with her grandpa, even if that home wasn't very far.

"Who, my mom?" Angeline asked. "Yeah, she's honest to a fault—which is why we didn't include her in this little game of ours."

I ran my hands through my snarled hair. "Your little game," I mumbled. "This whole thing was just a game."

For the first time in several days, I let myself sit back, relax, and think about my life before. Before I'd wound up at a math camp. Before I'd found that creepy note. Before I'd been tricked into thinking that some crazy killer was picking us off one by one. It was like I'd been dipped in plaster and set on a shelf to harden, but now the truth had set me free.

The whole thing was just a game.

Angeline wasn't dead.

Toby had never been kidnapped.

"But his voicemail," I peeped. "He said that I couldn't call home."

"Whose voicemail?" Angeline asked.

"Toby's voicemail!" I replied. "He disappeared the day after you did. They said he went into town, but then he never came back. Then his truck disappeared, and then he left me this voicemail that made it sound like he'd been captured."

She held her hand out. "Give it to me."

"Why do you want it?" I replied.

"So I can fix the stupid thing!"

I hesitated for a moment, then, finally, gave my phone to her. She tapped a bunch of buttons, pressed the phone against her ear, and listened carefully. Then, after taking out the battery and snapping it back in, she returned the phone to me.

"You should password-protect your in-box, but the voicemail's less garbled now."

Tentatively, I raised it to my ear. "Esther, I got your message. Your mom drove up to get me, and then we came back for the truck. You don't need to worry about *Westinghouse's Resting Place*. Concentrate on those classes, and *don't call home again.* You need to enjoy yourself."

I felt my cheeks get hot, but before I could come up with a suitable response, Angeline said, "See? Everything's fine."

At least that got my goat. "Everything's fine?" I fired back. "Was everything fine when Munch almost fell off a balcony? And was everything fine when I thought your grandpa was gonna shoot me in the back?"

Angeline flinched again. "I'm sorry. I really am. I guess I didn't think you guys would take everything so seriously."

But that wasn't good enough. "Why'd you do it?" I demanded.

"I already told you!" she replied. "You solved the First Problem in less than twenty-four hours! Do you have any idea how rare that is? When I told Archimedes how you solved it, he thought we should figure out what else your brain could do."

The aforementioned Archimedes, who'd been stirring spoonfuls of creamed corn into a can of stewed tomatoes, looked up from his colorful concoction. "Leave me out of this," he grumbled. "It was your idea, not mine."

"Maybe," she admitted. "But you were the one who got me started on logic puzzles in the first place." She set her sights on me. "I've been totally *obsessed* ever since Archimedes lent me his copy of *The Game of Logic.* It's written by the guy who wrote *Alice's Adventures in Wonderland*, but it's way more interesting."

I rolled my eyes. "I'm sure." Mixing math with the White Rabbit was bound to cause a few problems.

She didn't take the bait. "So I decided to design my very own logic puzzle—with Archimedes's help, of course."

He pointed his spoon at her head. "You keep trying to involve me, but I won't be involved. This mess is all yours, darlin'."

She managed to ignore him. "After I heard that you and Toby were headed back down to your truck, I left my little note where I was sure that you would see it. And once I had the clues, it was child's play to hide them." She stuck out her chin. "I've been playing in these woods since before I could subtract."

I glanced down at my toes. "I thought you and Graham were sneaking off."

"Is that because *you* wanted to sneak off with Graham?" she asked.

I felt my cheeks get hot again, but if there was one thing I'd learned from fencing, it was that sometimes the best defense was an even better offense. "So that *was* you in the woods earlier."

She lowered her gaze. "I didn't mean to get caught. I'm usually much stealthier." She held up her arm, which was sporting a Scooby-Doo Band-Aid. "When my cardigan snagged on a branch, I had to leave it behind."

"I *knew* Director Verity recognized your sweater!"

"I'm sure she did," Angeline said. "But she'd never give me away. She knows the other kids treat me differently when they know the truth."

"When they don't think you're dead, you mean."

She had the decency to blush, but then, I couldn't really blame her. Kids could be awful sometimes.

"What about the cipher?" I asked.

Her nose crinkled. "What cipher?"

"The cipher you posted in the common room." I looked

around the room for a printer. "Did you print it off here, or did you sneak into your mom's office?"

She held up both hands. "Honestly, Esther, I have no idea what you're talking about. I've been using this old typewriter I found out in the shed."

"Well, if it's not your cipher, then whose it is?" I replied.

She didn't have a chance to answer before someone pounded on the door. "Police!" a rough voice shouted. "If you don't open this door, I'm gonna have to break it down!"

CHAPTER 25

Now it was Angeline's turn to leap out of her seat. "What are the police doing here?" she asked as she looked back and forth between us.

Archimedes shook his head—his mouth was full of his concoction—but when Angeline tried to get the door, I jumped into her way.

"Let me get it," I replied. "I think I know what's going on."

I should have known that Graham wouldn't be able to keep his mouth shut. Luckily, I'd seen enough *Castle* that I knew what to do from here. After creeping past the lumpy couch, I opened the door oh-so-carefully and stuck both hands in the air. The cops didn't have their weapons drawn, but better to be safe than sorry.

The first cop had a handlebar mustache that wouldn't

have looked out of place in the Wild West. "Are you Archimedes?" he demanded.

"No, I'm Esther," I said. "You know, the murder victim? Except I'm still alive, so your services won't be required."

Captain Mustache and his partner exchanged a serious look. It was a look I'd seen a hundred times. They might as well have asked, *What are we supposed to do with* this *one?*

I patted my cheeks, then rubbed my stomach. "See, I'm not a ghost, so you can call off the SWAT team."

Captain Mustache shook his head. "I'm very sorry, miss, but I'm afraid I have to ask you to step out of the house." He glanced over my shoulder. "Are you home alone?"

I started to answer, then changed my mind at the last second. If I squealed on Archimedes, they might arrest him first and ask questions later, but he couldn't go to jail. He might starve without his peaches.

I was still trying to decide exactly what to tell the cops when a hand landed on my shoulder. I didn't have to turn around to know it belonged to Archimedes.

"I guess our jig is up," he said as he stepped out of the house. After closing the door behind us, he calmly held up his hands. "Please forgive my newfound friend for disrupting your evening, but allow me to explain."

He went on, of course, but I was no longer listening. I was scanning the edge of the clearing, looking for signs of the math nerds. As if on cue, a row of heads popped up from behind a distant bush.

"It's all right!" I shouted.

Munch lurched to his feet. "Esther?"

Before I could reply, two pairs of hands pulled him back down.

"It's all right!" I said again. "But we got it all wrong—"

"I'm very sorry, miss," Captain Mustache interrupted, "but I'm afraid I have to ask you to restrain yourself."

What was this guy, a robot? Luckily, before Captain Mustache could force me to calm down, Munch jerked out of Graham's grip and literally leaped over the bush. For a kid who could eat his weight in Swiss Rolls, he was pretty light on his feet.

"We thought you were dead!" Munch said.

Captain Mustache and his partner sharply spun around. Their hands flew to their holsters, but when they saw it was just Munch, they lowered their arms and went back to scowling.

"I'm not dead," I replied. "And I know what happened to Angeline and Toby!"

By the time the cops decided that Archimedes didn't have a bunch of bodies in his freezer, the sun had set completely, so we had to walk back to the lodge in the fading twilight. My flashlight couldn't compete with Captain Mustache's Maglite (which probably doubled as a nightstick), but I didn't turn it off. I liked the way it illuminated my path as we headed down the hill, our footsteps thumping in time with the flashlights' bouncing beams.

Archimedes opted to hang out at his cabin, but Angeline agreed to go back to the lodge with us. I wanted to grill her about the cipher, but Captain Mustache kept sending me these weird glances, so I kept my mouth shut.

The lodge shone like a beacon at the bottom of the hill. It helped that two squad cars were standing guard in the driveway, their headlights blazing. I thought Director Verity would be pacing on the porch, but she was just standing there glaring. At least her toe wasn't tapping, but then, you could only tap your toe so long before your shins gave out.

I was the one whose life had been on the line, but Director Verity's eyes were stuck on Angeline. "Do you have any idea how angry I am?" she demanded.

Angeline looked down at her toes. "Probably pretty angry," she mumbled.

"I'm *furious*," she said, but instead of lecturing her daughter, she yanked Angeline into a hug.

Angeline didn't protest, and Director Verity didn't cry, but that was probably just because she'd smashed her mascara-smeared face into her daughter's bony shoulder.

When Angeline pulled away, Director Verity sniffed. "I should have known it was *your* puzzle."

Angeline massaged her check (which was now sporting a dent from her mom's starched lapel). "I *told* you they'd kill it."

Director Verity half laughed, half sobbed. "I suppose you did," she said, smoothing Angeline's blond hair. "But I didn't think you were into ciphers."

Angeline shook her head. "Esther said something about a cipher, too, but I still don't know what you're talking about."

An alarm bell went off in my head—I was missing something here, something right under my nose—but before I could put my finger on it, Federico squinted into the twilight.

"Hey, isn't that Mr. Pearson?"

I craned my neck to see what he was squinting at, and sure enough, there was Mr. Pearson, who'd just rounded the corner with a knapsack on his back. He was weaving through the gaps between the squad cars' slashing headlights when, at the sound of his own name, he took off like a bottle rocket, his knapsack bouncing wildly.

Captain Mustache aimed his Maglite in Mr. Pearson's direction. "You there—stop!" he shouted.

But Mr. Pearson didn't stop; if anything, he picked up speed. Acting purely on instinct, I picked up a fallen branch—it was shorter than my foil, but it would have to do—and threw myself into his path.

"En garde!" I shouted as I got down into my squat.

He shuddered to a halt and cocked his head to the side, like he was trying to decide if I was serious. I was. I gave him a few seconds to pick up his own fallen branch, then, when he just stood there gaping, launched my preemptive assault.

I was going less for points than a swift and sudden take-down, so my form was less than perfect. When I lunged for his chest, he frantically blocked me with both arms, and when he tried to sidestep me, I cut him off with a smooth slide. In an effort to distract him, I slipped my branch under the strap of what I assumed was his knapsack and swiftly flung it off his shoulder. When he scrambled after it, I swept his feet out from under him. He landed on his back with a less-than-graceful *thud*.

While the math nerds clapped and cheered, I dragged myself back to my feet. The barrel-chested cop who'd been defending the squad cars gently rolled Mr. Pearson over and clapped handcuffs on his wrists. But I was much more interested in Mr. Pearson's gray knapsack. The flap had come undone, revealing a collection of loosely rolled can-vases. Frowning, I bent down so I could get a closer look. If I hadn't known better, I would have thought that they were paint—

"You're not going to believe this," Officer Bunyan

interrupted, "but I think we just caught the so-called Fenimore Forger."

Captain Mustache's jaw dropped.

"Who's the Fenimore Forger?" Brooklyn asked at the same time Graham said, "Fenimor!"

I couldn't help but raise my eyebrows. "You've heard of the Fenimore Forger?"

"Not really," Graham admitted, "but 'Fenimor' was the keyword we tried to tell you about earlier. It didn't mean anything to Marshane or me—"

"But it means something to us now," Marshane added for good measure.

And just like that, the pieces slid into place. Mr. Pearson was the Fenimore Forger. It explained the meaning of the cipher and his general creepiness. It even explained the old easel in the storage room. He'd been using the camp as a hideout, and now he'd gone and gotten himself apprehended.

We might not have caught a mass murderer, but we'd caught the Fenimore Forger, and that was almost as good.

Captain Mustache cleared his throat. "My apologies, Ms. Verity, but I'm afraid that I'm gonna need statements from you and all of your campers." Then he glanced at Keith, who'd fallen asleep on Graham's shoulder. The thin line of drool dangling out of his mouth was an especially nice touch. "But I guess we can come back and get those statements in the morning."

Director Verity nodded. "Thank you, Captain Williams."

Captain Mustache nodded, too. "Get some rest," he told us as he trudged back toward his car. When his gaze landed on me, his handlebar mustache twitched. "It sounds like you've had quite a day."

I hugged my sketchbook to my chest. "You have no idea."

CHAPTER 26

After subjecting us to a fake murder mystery and a real arrest, Director Verity decided to cut our session short. She called our parents first thing the next morning, so by the time we stumbled out of bed, a line of mud-encrusted minivans had already pulled into the driveway under the CAMP ARCHIMEDES sign. Brooklyn and Oliver were gone before breakfast was even served.

True to their word, the cops showed up after breakfast, unrolling yellow tape and demanding witness statements from the campers who hadn't left already. It was the first time I'd been a part of an official police investigation, so it was hard not to be inspired. I parked myself in the common room and sketched Captain Mustache's mustache and Director Verity's heels. As soon as I got home, I'd transfer these treasures to canvas, but before I left, I had one more thing to do.

Once Captain Mustache dismissed us, I corralled the rest of my team. Officer Bunyan was now guarding the storage room (though whether this was a step up or a step down from guarding the squad cars, I couldn't have said), so by unspoken agreement, we headed up the hill.

Despite the broken rocking chair, the inside of the shed wasn't as sinister in daylight. While Angeline sat on the workbench and Federico wiggled his way *under* the rocking chair, I committed the whole scene to memory. Toby said that art was just memories made physical, so if I wanted to make art, I had to make memories first.

"So why'd you drag us up here?" Marshane finally asked.

At least that snapped me out of it. Slowly, very slowly, I pulled out the sketchbook. "It's all here," I said softly, setting it down on the workbench. It landed with a dull *thump*.

The others leaned over the sketchbook like it was some kind of holy relic.

"All the puzzles, all the doodles, all the right—and wrong—guesses." A lump of pure nostalgia got caught at the back of my throat. "It's a work of art itself."

Federico snorted. "Don't get mushy on us *now*."

"Fair enough," I said as I nudged the sketchbook toward them. "But I think someone else should keep it."

Graham's eyes bulged. "No way." He pushed the sketch-book back toward me.

I pushed it back toward him. "*Yes* way."

Munch eyed the sketchbook like he thought it might sting. "But how will you remember?"

"How could I forget?" I asked. "Besides, as soon as I get home, I'm gonna paint you guys into a mural." I stuck my chin out at the sketchbook. "So I'm not gonna need *that*."

An uncomfortable silence settled over the room. Shoes squeaked. Stomachs growled. No one wanted to look greedy, or maybe no one wanted it, period. I resisted the urge to sneak it back under my shirt. That would only make it worse.

Finally, Angeline broke the silence. "Why don't we *all* keep it?" she asked. "Everyone could tear out their own page."

I drew a shallow breath. Despite Mom's best efforts, Toby and I had never been churchgoing folks, so in our opinion, defacing works of art was the most irreverent thing that you could do. But I'd misjudged the other math nerds, so maybe I was misjudging this, too. Maybe it wasn't defacing. Maybe it was simply sharing.

Without saying a word, I tore the page with Sphinx's note out of the sketchbook, then passed it to Angeline, who tore out the next page. She passed it to Federico, who handed it to Munch. After adding a few chocolaty fingerprints, Munch passed it to Graham. Happiness glowed in my chest as I watched the sketchbook make the rounds. We weren't rewriting history, but we were writing *our* history, and that was even better.

By the time it reached Marshane, the sketchbook looked visibly lighter. Federico hadn't quite gotten his whole page out of the sketchbook, so a small clump of paper was still clinging to the binding. A part of me wanted to grab it and protect it from more damage, but I held that part at bay.

Marshane thumbed through the pages and cocked an eyebrow at me, but I didn't react. A rise was what he wanted, so I held my peace.

"Call me greedy," Marshane said as he tore out the rest of the pages. After folding them in half and tucking them into his pocket, he returned the sketchbook to me.

I might have been the first person to wound it, but holding those two pieces of cardboard between my calloused fingers nearly did me in. Angeline must have been able to tell that I was about to cry, because she hopped off the workbench and yanked it out of my hands.

"To the number crunchers!" she said brashly as she raised the sketchbook high.

Federico crawled out from under the rocking chair. "To the killer!" he added.

Marshane took advantage of Angeline's blush to rip the sketchbook out of her hands. "You know, it's really too bad we can't set this thing on fire. That's how you put Jedi to rest."

She tossed her hair over her shoulder. "Who says we can't?" she asked.

"Won't we get in trouble?" Graham replied. It was like he thought Captain Mustache—or, worse, Director Verity—had long-range X-ray vision.

Angeline waved that off. "It's a campfire," she said. "And this is a summer camp."

Marshane ruffled Graham's red hair. "What's the worst thing that could happen?"

"We could start a forest fire."

Munch nodded solemnly. "We could get ourselves stranded."

Angeline bumped me in the shoulder. "Even if we do, we'll have Esther here to save us."

I liked the sound of that.

Acknowledgments

First, thank you to Brent Taylor, who read this book over a weekend, then made an enthusiastic offer. This math nerd couldn't have found a more adept advocate.

Second, thank you to Allison Moore, who polished this book until it shone. If you loved this book any less than the ones that you acquired, you never let it show. Also, thank you to Brett Wright, who originally brought this book to Bloomsbury, and to the whole Bloomsbury team, especially Mary Kate Castellani and Liz Byer.

I couldn't have written this book without my awesome critique partners, especially Liesl Shurtliff, Michelle Mason, and Myrna Foster. Your comments gave this story the initial push it needed (and Myrna, you were right—it definitely needed one more puzzle). Thanks also to Ashley Turcotte, who read several synopses for this book at practically a moment's notice.

Another thank-you to my parents, Gary and Linda Van Dolzer, for their ceaseless support. Thanks also to Kate Testerman for her feedback on early drafts, to Jason Keeley for his expertise on puzzles of all sorts, and to David Richard Garner for his help brainstorming ideas (even if I didn't end up using most of them).

Last but never least, another huge thank-you to Chris, who contributed not just moral support but his mad problem-solving skills, and to Isaac, Madeleine, and William, whose love for all things math makes this mom all kinds of happy. I hope your little sister loves math as much as you and I do.

J
Van Dolzer, Krista,
The multiplying mysteries of Mount
 Ten /

Apr 2019